# MUSLIM GIRL

## a novel

*To Yasmin. May the book be a joy + inspiration.*

# Umm Zakiyyah

*5/28/2016*

**AL-WALAA**
PUBLICATIONS

# MUSLIM GIRL

a novel by Umm Zakiyyah

ISBN 10:  0970766785
ISBN 13:  9780970766786

Library of Congress Control Number: 2013935444

Order information available online at
**muslimfiction.com** and **ummzakiyyah.com**

Published by Al-Walaa Publications
Camp Springs, Maryland  USA

Printed in the USA

Cover photography by Shutterstock.com ®
Front cover photo copyright by Darrin Henry
Back cover photo copyright by Dustin Dennis

# Glossary of Arabic Terms

*abaya:* large outer garment for Muslim women

*Allah:* the Arabic term for "God"

*Allahu'akbar:* proclamation of the greatness of God, often expressed in excitement or happiness

*As-salaamu'alaikum:* the Muslim greeting of peace, literally "peace be upon you," often said in place of "hello" and "goodbye" and is sometimes extended to include *wa-rahmatullaah* and/or *wa-barakaatuh*

*Astaghfirullah:* expression said upon committing a mistake or sin or upon hearing or witnessing something sinful or reprehensible, literally "I seek God's forgiveness"

*daff:* small hand drum

*da'wah:* any teaching about Islam for the purpose of clarifying religious misunderstandings or inviting someone to become Muslim

*deen:* religion, often used in reference to the religion of Islam

*du'aa:* supplication to God or informal prayer

*jilbaab:* outer garment for Muslim women that resembles a large, loose dress, sometimes used in reference to the Saudi-style abaya

*insha'Allah:* literally "if God wills" or "God-willing," often said in reference to something expected or hoped to happen in the future

*kaafir:* disbeliever

*khimaar:* Muslim woman's head cover, often referred to as *hijab*

*maashaAllah:* literally "it was God's will," often said in admiration of something or in acceptance of a situation

*niqaab:* face veil

*Qur'an:* the Muslim holy book

*shahaadah:* the Muslim testimony of faith, formally recited to officially enter the religion of Islam

*SubhaanAllah:* glorification of the greatness and perfection of God, often uttered upon sudden inspiration, epiphany, or surprise

*Sunnah:* the exemplary prophetic example drawn from the life, sayings, and teachings of Prophet Muhammad, peace be upon him

*ukhti:* term of friendly endearment for females, literally means "my sister"

*Wa'aliku-mus-salaam:* the Muslim greeting of peace said in response to *As-salaamu'alaikum* and is sometimes extended to include *wa-rahmatullaah* and/or *wa-barakaatuh*

*Wallah:* an oath in the name of God, literally "By God," often uttered to emphasize the truth of something

*wudhoo:* ritual ablution before formal prayers

# DEDICATION

*For those who are making peace with who they are—*
*and embracing, ever so furtively,*
*who they can become*

*I don't know how this journey will end.*
*I don't even know fully where I stand.*
*I know only that I have faith. And for me,*
*that's all that matters now.*

—from the journal of Umm Zakiyyah

# PROLOGUE

*When my mother became Muslim, I didn't even know what a Muslim was. I mean, what does a nine-year-old know about religion?*

*I remember when she first told me. I was tucking the* Ebony *magazine under my pillow so that my parents wouldn't know I was reading it. I looked up and saw my mother standing near my bedroom door. Her arms were folded, and she was frowning, looking all upset. I thought she was angry with me for reading "grown-up stuff," but she just sat on the edge of my bed and smiled at me.*

*"Naya, I'm Muslim now." Her eyes seemed sad for some reason.*

*"What?"*

*"I'm Muslim." Her smile seemed childlike, like she was waiting for my approval.*

*I averted my gaze and pulled the covers up to my shoulders as I settled under them. "Okay." I had no idea what she was talking about, but since I was pretty sure I wasn't in trouble, I just wanted to go to sleep.*

*My mother stood and patted my head. "Thanks, Naya." She turned off the light and closed the door as she left. I lay awake in the darkness for several minutes before finally shutting my eyes and drifting to sleep.*

*"Children are resilient." That's what my father used to say. Maybe that's why I jumped head-on into Islam myself and even learned Arabic and Qur'an and thought it was "cool" to live in Saudi Arabia.*

Oh my God.

*Did I really think that?*

# 1

# The Move

"Well, it's definitely not what we had in mind when we moved here," Veronica said, the cordless phone between her shoulder and ear as she kneeled down to pick up a stack of books from the floor. She wiped a hand on her jeans before standing and shuffling through the old paperbacks. "At this point, we have no idea where he's going to find work in Maryland. All we know is we can't live here anymore." She grunted, wrinkling her nose as she tossed a wilted, coverless book to the pile on the floor. "At least if we plan to stay married."

Inaya stood on the opposite side of the living room, hands on her hips as she surveyed the clutter. Dust soiled the faded white T-shirt that she wore, and the worn threads in the right knee of her jeans exposed brown skin in need of lotion.

Inaya bit her lower lip as she looked at the piles of glass plates, bowls, and cups. She glanced uncertainly at her mother, who was leaning over a box and arranging some books inside. The faded black handkerchief knotted at the back of Veronica's head exposed an array of short twists that were fraying at the ends.

"That's what we thought too," Veronica said, amusement in her tone. "You'd expect a bit more from a Muslim country, huh? But they just couldn't get over the idea of an Arab guy marrying a black woman."

"Mom?" Inaya knew it was better to wait till her mother finished talking before asking about the dishes, but her stepfather had said he wanted everything packed by the time he returned from work.

Veronica brought a hand to her mouth to stifle laughter, a clear sign she hadn't heard Inaya speaking to her. "Girl, you're a trip," Veronica said, shaking her head. "I threw away most of my old pictures. But to tell you the truth, Sa'ad wanted to keep the ones from graduate school."

"Mom?" Inaya's raised voice was on the verge of a whine.

"Hold on a second." Veronica covered the mouthpiece with one hand and turned toward Inaya.

"What is it?"

"What should I do with the dishes?"

"Pack them. What else?"

"But they're glass. Won't they break?"

"Get some old newspaper and wrap them."

Inaya's eyes widened. "Each one?"

Veronica drew her eyebrows together in annoyance. "Yes. Each one. Now, hurry up before Sa'ad gets home."

"But…"

Veronica was already turned back around and engaged in conversation before Inaya could protest further.

"Girl, you know I gave up modeling after I became Muslim," Veronica said, her grin visible as Inaya sighed and went to retrieve an empty box. "That was the first thing Sa'ad told me after he asked to marry me." She laughed. "But he said there's no harm in keeping a few pictures."

Inaya groaned as she dropped the empty box on the floor next to the dishes then dragged herself to the kitchen to find old newspapers.

A faint cry came from a back room as Inaya crouched in front of a cabinet near the sink. She pulled a stack of aged *Arab News* and *Saudi Gazette* papers from the bottom shelf and set them on the floor.

"Inaya," Veronica called from the living room, "can you bring me the baby?"

Sighing, Inaya pushed herself to a standing position, then reached over the sink and held one palm up as she pressed the soap dispenser with the other. She rubbed her palms together to distribute the white cream over both hands before turning on the tap and letting the water run over her hands. She would have to find a clean shirt to change into too. Her mother was very particular about never handling a newborn with soiled clothing and dirty hands.

***

"Surprise!"

Inaya's eyes widened as she surveyed the large room that was filled with dozens of girls she had met during the seven years she had lived in Riyadh. Amongst them were Saudi girls she had tutored in English or met at school, as well as expats from India, Pakistan, America, and the United Kingdom whom she had befriended or met during an Arabic or Qur'an class.

Inaya laughed and glanced behind her at her mother, and Veronica grinned back at Inaya, the baby against Veronica's chest from where she stood in the doorway of the small house. The rest of the women, mothers of most of the girls, relaxed outside on blankets spread out on grass patches atop the dirt and sand. The expansive land was enclosed by a tall stone wall that afforded the women maximum privacy when they removed their abayas and veils.

"You have fun," Veronica said, squeezing Inaya's arm gently, one arm cradling the baby. "I'm outside if you need me."

Inaya nodded as her mother released her arm and turned the door handle to go outside. Inaya was yanked into the crowd by one of her friends before she could respond.

"Were you surprised?" Rafa said, looping her arm through Inaya's and guiding Inaya across the room. Rafa's dark eyes sparkled as she looked eagerly at Inaya.

Inaya laughed. "I had no idea. My mom just said we should take a break from packing."

5

The other girls squealed in laughter, clapping their hands together. "Your mom is so cool, *maashaAllah*," Rafa said, grinning.

"Did she help plan this?" Inaya's eyes widened more as she looked at her friends.

Rafa nodded. "It was her idea."

"No way…"

"We wanted to do something for you before you left," Rafa said. "So we asked her opinion."

"My mom is a trip." Inaya smiled knowingly as she unhooked her arm from Rafa's. Inaya lifted her chin slightly as she unfastened the pin of her *khimaar*. She pulled at the black chiffon cloth, exposing the mass of braids that framed her face. "She had me thinking we were going to be cleaning the house all night."

The rhythmic sound of a drum came from a far corner of the room, and Inaya turned to see two of her Saudi friends beating a small drum and nodding their heads to the rhythm.

"*Yaa ukhtunaa,*" they sang in harmony, "*nuhibbuki fillaah. Yaa ukhutunaa, hafidhakillaah…*" *O our sister, we love you for the sake of Allah. O our sister, may you be under the protection of Allah…*

Rafa grabbed Inaya's hands and began to dance playfully. The other girls laughed and jumped to their feet and joined in as the Saudi girls continued to play the *daff* and sing.

\*\*\*

"The first thing I want to say, Inaya, is that you're an inspiration to all of us, *maashaAllah*." The Saudi girls who had been singing and playing the drum now stood in front of the room as the other girls sat on the Arab-style floor couch that lined the room's walls, looking at the sisters as the elder one spoke. Tears glistened in Batool's eyes as she gazed at Inaya.

"I'm really sad to see you go," Batool said, "*Wallah*, before I met you, I took the Qur'an for granted. And I took Arabic for granted too. But seeing you memorize the whole Qur'an and push everyone to learn Arabic, *subhaanAllah*, it made me realize how important Qur'an and *Fus-ha* should be in our lives."

Batool's younger sister nodded her head, her expression thoughtful.

"I remember when I first met you," Batool said, smiling sadly, "and I asked why you want to learn Arabic when you already have the best language in the world."

Inaya smiled at the memory, bowing her head from where she sat next to Rafa on the floor couch, a half-eaten plate of food on the carpet by her feet.

"And you said, 'No, *you* have the best language in the world. What can be better than the language of Qur'an?'"

Batool shook her head as she drew in a deep breath. "*Wallah*, hearing you say that made me so ashamed, and after that I started memorizing Qur'an myself."

\*\*\*

*We have no idea what we're going to do without you,*
*"The girl who gets things done."*
*But I suppose we'll have to figure out a way to still learn,*
*Do things right, and have some fun!*
*Thanks for teaching us the meaning of friendship*
*And love for Allah's sake.*
*Thanks for telling us to pray and cover—*
*Without taking a break!*
*Thanks for teaching us that Islam is a religion of action,*
*Not a religion of words.*
*Thanks for reminding us that saying*

*No! to Allah (about anything) is absurd.*
*We're going to miss you, Inaya,*
*Our beloved sister, "cousin", and friend.*
*But like you always say, "Keep the faith, girl,*
*And, insha'Allah, we'll meet in the End."*

Inaya smiled as she sat on the edge of her bed late that night, re-reading the poem the girls had written and given to her.

"Are you nervous about going back to America?" Rafa had asked her.

Inaya had laughed. "Honestly, I can't wait."

"Really?" Her friend seemed genuinely surprised.

"I'm going to miss everyone," Inaya said. "But I look forward to having a normal life again."

Inaya folded the paper and stuffed it back into the envelope before setting it on top of her other cards and gifts next to her bed. She stood and reached across the pile to press the light switch by the door. The room went black, and Inaya felt a lump in her throat.

"Are you going to come back to visit?" Rafa had asked as she helped Inaya put the gifts in the back of the car.

"My mom says we'll probably never come back," Inaya said as she pushed some boxes to the side to make room for others.

When Inaya turned to take a bag from Rafa, she saw Rafa's eyes widen through the slit of the black veil. "Never?"

Inaya shook her head. "She said we did Hajj and 'Umrah, and that's enough."

"But what about Brother Sa'ad? He won't visit his family?"

Inaya shrugged. "A lot of his family live in Virginia, so I'm not sure."

"But…"

Inaya waved her hand. "I guess he can come by himself if he wants."

"No way… You won't come too?"

Inaya was silent momentarily. "I'm not sure I want to."

Rafa averted her gaze and was quiet as she helped Inaya arrange the last of the gifts in the trunk. The embrace she gave Inaya minutes later was devoid of its normal emotion, and Inaya sensed something she had said cut her friend deep.

Inaya pulled the bedcovers over herself and recited *Ayatul-Kursi* in the dark. She shut her eyes and tried to concentrate on the verses of Qur'an, but Inaya could still see Rafa's sad eyes avoiding hers.

A second later Inaya thought of her father and friends in America, and Inaya's heart swelled in anticipation for her flight back home next week.

# 2

# America

"Too many rules," Anthony said in response to his younger sister, who stood next to him on the balcony of the suburban Maryland home that their parents owned. He tapped his cigarette lightly against the wooden railing before bringing it to his mouth.

"Then don't follow the rules," Veronica said. "That's better than never becoming Muslim."

Anthony's gaze was thoughtful as he exhaled a train of smoke. "That's new."

"What's new?" Veronica turned to her brother, her eyebrows drawn together.

"Making compromises." He frowned momentarily. "It was always all or nothing with you."

She creased her forehead. "I never said that."

"You didn't have to. You always come here preaching like God asked us to be angels or else we'll burn in Hell."

Veronica drew in a deep breath as her gaze rested on the grass and trees aligning the fence of the backyard. How could she respond to something like that? Sometimes she felt it didn't matter what she said or did. She would be viewed negatively as long as she was Muslim.

"And according to you," Anthony said, "God makes the rules, so we have no choice but to follow them."

Veronica sighed. "We always have a choice, Tony. There are just consequences for what we choose."

"Then why are you telling me to break rules?"

"I didn't mean it like that. I meant it's better to be a sinful Muslim than to not be Muslim at all."

Anthony was silent as he squinted his eyes and smoked.

"Look, Tony," Veronica said, "Muslims aren't angels. Nobody's able to follow the rules perfectly."

Anthony grunted, a smug grin on his face. "You seem to be doing a pretty good job."

"Oh please." Veronica waved her hand. "I'm far from perfect."

"You don't act like it."

"Why? Because I speak up when something's wrong?"

"You make people uncomfortable," Anthony said after a thoughtful pause. "You need to realize that."

Veronica was quiet momentarily. "I realize Islam isn't the most comfortable subject."

Anthony leaned on the railing, the cigarette dangling between two fingers. "What happened with you and Chris?"

At the mention of her ex-husband, Veronica's heart constricted. Chris had been her high school sweetheart, and in the innocence of youth, they had vowed to always be together. Chris had proposed to Veronica the day of their high school graduation, and, teary-eyed, she'd accepted.

Veronica sighed. "Tony, you already know the answer to that."

Anthony looked at his sister. "You really hurt him, you know that?"

Veronica looked away from her brother. "It wasn't easy for me either."

Anthony brought the cigarette to his mouth then blew out a cloud of smoke. He tapped the cigarette on the railing as he stood upright. "Chris started studying religion after you left."

Veronica drew in a deep breath, uncomfortable with the conversation, but she didn't know what to say.

Anthony chuckled to himself. "And he came across something that really got to him."

Anthony was quiet for several seconds as he smoked.

"What?" Veronica said quietly, glancing at her brother.

"It was about a man who wanted to marry a woman," Anthony said, prompting Veronica to look away. "And she said no because she was Muslim and he was a pagan."

There was a long pause.

"But she finally agreed to marry him."

Veronica's eyes widened, unable to hide her shock as she looked at Anthony. "Really?"

"And she didn't want money or a ring or anything," Anthony said, a slight smile on his face, but it was clear his thoughts were elsewhere. "She just asked him for one thing."

Veronica narrowed her eyes as the story began to sound vaguely familiar. She recalled reading a similar story in Arabian history. "What's that?"

"That he become Muslim so they could be together."

Veronica's heart grew heavy and she averted her gaze. Yes, she knew the story after all. It was the famous story of Abu Talha and Umm Sulaim.

Anthony and Veronica were quiet for some time.

"But what about Inaya?" Anthony said, looking at his sister, concern in his eyes.

Veronica furrowed her brows as she looked at her brother. "What do you mean?"

"How does she feel about all this?"

Veronica felt herself growing defensive. "All of what?"

"You don't get it, do you?" Anthony shook his head. "You walk around as if everything you do is right for everyone else. I just hope you don't lose your daughter in the process."

Veronica glared at her brother. She started to respond, but Anthony spoke before she could.

"I swear, every time I see that girl, I feel sorry for her. She has no identity."

"She's Muslim, Tony. That's identity enough."

"For *you*," he said. "Don't forget, she didn't choose Islam. You did."

"She loves being Muslim, Tony. In many ways, she's stronger than I am."

"I don't doubt that, Ronnie. I just wonder if it's only because she wants to make you happy."

Veronica rolled her eyes. "I think you just have a hard time understanding how a sixteen-year-old can be stronger than you."

Anthony coughed laughter. "Most youth are stronger than people my age, if you ask me. Once you hit forty, you aren't trying to change your lifestyle, even if it's the right thing to do."

He tapped his cigarette against the railing again. "But this has nothing to do with me. I was just hoping you'd be more concerned about Inaya than your pride."

\*\*\*

"Eww…" Inaya wrinkled her nose as she read the label of the container her cousin had just handed her. "Margarine? Are you trying to kill us? Where's the butter?"

"What's wrong with margarine?" Kayla said as she took the container from Inaya and carried it back to the refrigerator.

"Are you kidding?" Inaya laughed. "It's not even a food substance."

Kayla groaned as she opened the refrigerator and put the margarine back inside. "Is this something else Muslims can't eat?"

Inaya rolled her eyes. "No. It's something humans can't eat, you included."

"I didn't know you guys were health nuts."

"We're not. I just want to live past forty."

"My dad is forty-four, and he eats margarine all the time."

"Kayla," Inaya said, sighing, "can you just pass me the butter? I'm craving chocolate chip cookies, and I want to be done before my mom announces we have to leave."

Kayla shut the refrigerator then set four sticks of butter on the kitchen table next to Inaya. "Can I help with anything?"

"You can crack the eggs."

"Is this some secret family recipe or something? Why can't I mix the batter?"

"If it was a secret, I wouldn't let you watch."

Inaya removed the foil wrapping from a stick of butter then set it on a glass plate before doing the same with the other sticks. "We'll have to microwave these for about twenty seconds. They need to be soft."

"The margarine was already soft," Kayla said, a half grin on her face as she carried the plate to the microwave. "We'd be halfway done if you weren't so picky."

"Things that are bad for you are always easier," Inaya said, flashing a smile. "It's better to be picky than sick."

The humming buzz of the microwave filled the silence between them.

"Is that why you guys are Muslim?" Kayla glanced hesitantly at her cousin. "You think being Christian was bad for us?"

Inaya creased her forehead as she looked at Kayla. "What? I'm talking about food, Kayla, not religion."

"I know. I'm just—" A beeping sound prompted Kayla to turn around and open the microwave. "I'm just wondering if that's why you guys left the church."

Inaya sighed as her cousin set the plate of butter in front of her. "I think it's more complicated than that, Kayla. My mom didn't just wake up and decide Christianity is bad for us."

"That's how is seems to us," Kayla said as she sat on a high stool and reached for the carton of eggs.

Inaya was silent as she used a rubber spatula to scrape the soft butter into the large mixing bowl. "You and I were only nine when my mom became Muslim."

"But don't you remember church?" Kayla smiled, lost in a pleasant memory. "We used to sit in the pew and pass notes during the service."

Inaya laughed beside herself. "Yeah, and then my mom would pinch me so hard I felt like screaming."

"Oh my God." Kayla shook her head. "Those sermons were so boring."

"I just went for the songs."

Kayla chuckled. "Girl, you went because your mom made you."

"Yeah," Inaya agreed, laughter in her voice. "Just like you."

"You don't miss church?" Kayla raised her voice over the sound of the electric mixer. She tapped the side of an egg on the small mixing bowl in front of her before pulling the shell open and emptying the whites and yolk inside the bowl.

Inaya shrugged as she steered the mixer around the bowl. "Not really. I mean, for me, there wasn't much to miss. I was too young to really care either way."

"I can't imagine my mom becoming Muslim. I think I'd freak out."

Inaya wore a smirk as she lifted her gaze to her cousin before looking at the mixture again. "Why?"

"I can't imagine giving up everything I love."

"Oh please, Kayla. It's not like that."

"Well, to me it is."

"How do you know? You've never been Muslim."

"I see Aunt Ronnie and you. It's like being a nun, except worse."

Inaya's eyes widened playfully. "Worse? You make it sound like religion is a punishment."

"Maybe it is."

Inaya glared at Kayla, but Inaya's pleasant expression remained.

"I sort of like the idea that Jesus died for my sins," Kayla said.

"But he didn't." Inaya turned off the electric mixer and set it on the table.

Kayla handed her the bowl of eggs. "Yeah, I know."

Taken aback, Inaya creased her forehead as she met Kayla's gaze. "And you still believe it?"

Kayla shrugged. "No, but I want to."

Inaya regarded her cousin skeptically. "Don't you think that's kind of hypocritical?"

"My dad says we're all hypocrites."

Inaya grunted laughter as she emptied the bowl of eggs into the butter-sugar mixture. "I don't think so."

"Well, maybe not you and Aunt Ronnie, but—"

"And what would make us the exception?" Inaya turned on the electric mixer and glanced curiously at Kayla as she maneuvered the mixer around the bowl.

"You're living what you believe," Kayla said, raising her voice again over the mixer.

"I thought your family believed all that stuff from church."

"We used to."

"Wait." Inaya drew her eyebrows together as she looked at her cousin. "You're saying the whole family doesn't even believe in Christianity?"

Kayla contorted her face. "Girl, I'm just talking about me and my parents."

"Aunt Sharon and Uncle Tony aren't Christian anymore?"

"Well, maybe my mom is," Kayla said thoughtfully. "But my dad doesn't go to church much these days."

"Why?"

Kayla shrugged. "He doesn't really talk about it. But Uncle Chris says it's because he's going through a spiritual crisis."

At the mention of her father, Inaya grew silent. She hadn't seen him since she arrived to America three weeks ago. They spoke briefly on the phone the day she arrived, but her mother hadn't had time to arrange a visit—at least that's what she said.

"And how does my dad know what Uncle Tony is going through?" Inaya's voice was devoid of the energy of seconds before, but she hoped her cousin didn't notice.

"They hang out a lot." Kayla chuckled. "Uncle Chris even took him to an open house at a mosque."

Inaya's eyes widened at she looked at Kayla. "What?"

Kayla creased her forehead as she met Inaya's gaze. "You didn't know your dad is thinking about converting?"

Inaya halted her motions and turned off the mixer. She set it on the table as she stared at Kayla in disbelief. "What?"

Kayla shrugged. "Maybe I misunderstood. But that's what my dad said."

Uncertain what to say, Inaya walked over to the counter and opened a cabinet. Her thoughts were distant as her eyes scanned the shelves.

*"Because he wasn't Muslim, sweetheart."* It was her mother's constant response to why she divorced Inaya's father. *"So it just couldn't work."*

Inaya's heart raced with hope. *What if...?* Inaya thought of her stepfather and her baby brother Abdullah, and she immediately felt ashamed of herself.

It could never happen, she thought sadly.

"The flour's on the table," Kayla said, humor in her tone.

Inaya started as she turned to Kayla. She had momentarily forgotten her cousin was in the kitchen.

"Oh yeah," Inaya said, an awkward smile on her face as she closed the cabinets and walked back to the table.

"You think he'll convert?" Kayla was looking curiously at Inaya.

Inaya contorted her face as she opened the bag of flour. "I don't know. He never mentioned it to me."

"I know, but…" Kayla's gaze grew distant. "But do you think he'd do it, you know?"

Inaya shrugged, her deflated hope making it difficult to pay full attention to her cousin. "If he wants to."

"But what about Dana?"

"What about her?" Inaya's tone was sarcastic. She didn't want to talk about her father's girlfriend. Inaya hated the way the woman always tried to be so sweet and polite whenever she talked to Inaya. But Inaya sensed Dana looked down on her and her mother because they were Muslim.

"Are you kidding?" Kayla said, laughter in her tone. "Dana is practically married to the church."

"And?" Inaya said, rolling her eyes. "My dad doesn't owe her anything. He can find someone else."

"After being together for four years?" Kayla chuckled. "Come on, Inaya. She's already talking about them getting married."

Inaya halted dipping a measuring cup into the flour as she regarded Kayla. "Did my dad say that?"

"No, I don't think so, but—"

"Then he can find someone else." Inaya resumed measuring out the flour and dumping it into the cookie batter.

In the silence that followed, Inaya felt Kayla studying her curiously.

"Yeah," Kayla said finally, but Inaya could hear the insincerity in her cousin's voice. "Maybe he can."

# 3

# A New School

It was a Monday morning in early September when Inaya followed Sa'ad and Veronica as they entered the glass double doors of the public school that Inaya would attend. Heart hammering in excitement, Inaya stared in awe at the massive main staircase and the ceiling-to-floor glass pillars displaying academic and athletic trophies, plaques, and medals. She slowed her steps to study the smiling faces in some of the framed pictures next to the awards.

"You can wait out here if you want," Veronica said, prompting Inaya to turn toward her mother, who was holding open the door to the front office across the hall. "We'll let you know if we need you."

"Okay." Inaya nodded as Veronica followed Sa'ad into the office, the door closing behind them.

Inaya walked slowly along the pillars, pausing to study the inscriptions on each award. *2nd Place National Varsity Cheerleading Competition. 1st Place Regional Spelling Bee Champions. Who's Who Among American High School Scholars. Distinguished Student Award, 2008. National Scholars Award, 2010. Award for Academic Excellence, 2009. Future Hope Scholars, 2011.*

"May I help you?"

Inaya started and found herself opposite a young man wearing a polite smile, his hands clasped near his waist.

Inaya didn't know what to say so she just stared at him.

"Are you a student here?" he asked, the polite smile still on his face. Inaya sensed that he thought she was violating a rule of some kind.

It was then that Inaya saw the badge attached to the left side of his dress shirt. "Student Ambassador."

His kind mannerisms and the walnut brown of his face held a vague sense of familiarity, but Inaya couldn't explain this feeling.

"If so, you need a hall pass during class times."

Inaya shook her head. "I'm not a student," she said finally. "My parents are in the office registering me for school."

His eyebrows rose in understanding. "Yes, of course." There was an awkward pause, as neither knew what to say.

"If you would like to take a look around," he said, "feel free. But you'll need a visitor's pass and a chaperone."

Inaya lifted her eyebrows. "A chaperone?"

He laughed lightly. "I know it sounds like a first date, but it's our school policy for visitors."

Inaya's cheeks grew warm, and she averted her gaze. "I'm sorry... I didn't know. I just..."

"No problem," he said, holding up a hand. "Just wait here for a moment."

Before Inaya could respond, he disappeared into an unlabeled door near the front office. He reappeared less than a minute later and handed her a badge similar to the one he was wearing. She hesitated momentarily then accepted it. "VISITOR" it said in all-red capital letters.

"Just pin it to your dress, and no one should bother you."

"Thanks..."

There was an awkward silence as she struggled with the safety pin affixed to the back of the plastic. When she was finally able to close the pin, the badge hung lopsided.

"Where are you from?"

Inaya heard the question as she frowned at the visitor badge. "I'm sorry?" Inaya said, as she glanced up at the student.

"You have an interesting accent," he said, his dark eyes kind as he looked at her. "I was just wondering where you're from."

Inaya's eyes widened slightly. "I do?"

The ambassador laughed heartily, and the long dimples in his cheeks made Inaya realize why he seemed familiar to her. He resembled the singer Usher, whose public divorce and court case she and her friends had followed in the internet news in Saudi Arabia.

"I'm sorry," he said, and it was then that Inaya realized his laugh was from embarrassment. "I didn't mean it offensively. It's just...Well, I thought you sounded Arab."

Inaya creased her forehead, unable to hide her amused expression. "Arab?"

His smile faded, but he tried to appear diplomatic. "I'm not good at judging ethnicities. It was just a wild guess."

"I'm American," Inaya said, unable to keep from chuckling. "But I suppose it makes sense." She shrugged. "My family just came back from Saudi Arabia."

"Cool." His wide smile returned. "Do you speak Arabic?"

Inaya nodded. "A bit."

"Maybe that's where the accent comes from."

Inaya was silent, unsure how she felt about having an Arab accent. She would have to be more careful when she spoke.

An awkward silence followed.

"Do you want to take a look around the school?" the student ambassador asked.

Inaya grinned. "I thought I needed a chaperone for that," she said, surprised by how comfortable she felt with him.

A smile spread on his face. "I could be your chaperone."

Inaya felt wary all of a sudden, but she maintained a pleasant expression.

"As a student ambassador," he added quickly, as if sensing her apprehension.

She glanced uncertainly at the door to the main office.

"We'll stay on this floor," he said.

"Okay…" she said reluctantly. "As long as we don't go far."

"No problem," he said with a smile. "It'll only take a minute."

Inaya bit her lower lip as a hesitant smile formed on her face. "That would be great. Thanks."

"Forgive me." He smiled and stuck out his hand. "I didn't introduce myself. I'm Raymond."

It took a moment for Inaya to realize that he was waiting for her to shake his hand. Her cheeks grew warm, and her heart pounded wildly in her chest.

"I'm Inaya," she said, her voice barely above a whisper. She tucked her hands deep into the pockets of her *jilbaab* and smiled widely at him.

Raymond's face registered confusion then embarrassment. He pulled his hand away. "I'm sorry. I forgot that you don't—"

"It's okay." Inaya felt so stupid. He probably thought she was an idiot.

Raymond appeared flustered, but a hesitant grin formed on his face as he started down the hall. "I guess I'm not the best chaperone, huh?"

Inaya was unsure how to respond, so she just fell in step next to him.

"This hall leads to the auditorium," he said as they rounded the corner. "That's where the ambassadors have their orientation."

There was an awkward silence, and Inaya glanced sideways at him.

"But I guess I didn't listen well to the instructions," he said with a smile, and Inaya sensed he was making a joke.

"Multicultural sensitivity training," he said, still smiling. "That's where the ambassadors learned about different cultures." He chuckled. "I forgot about the *Wahhabi* sect."

His tone was apologetic. "We don't have a lot of fundamentalists at the school."

Inaya winced and her cheeks burned in offense. She was so upset that she couldn't look at him.

"Is everything okay?"

"Yes," she murmured, her heart pounding in nervous anger. "But I'm not a fundamentalist."

Raymond knitted his eyebrows in confusion. "I'm sorry. I just assumed…"

"You shouldn't assume." Inaya's voice was tight.

Raymond remained silent, and Inaya sensed he had no idea what he'd done wrong.

Inaya was suddenly self-conscious of the black *khimaar* that framed her face and the wide black over-garment that she was sure looked like a stupid oversized dress.

A classroom door opened in front of them and they halted their steps as a girl and boy emerged holding hands. The girl was leaning her head on the boy's shoulder, but when her eyes met Inaya's, the girl lifted her head and wrinkled her nose.

"What the hell is that?" the girl said in a harsh whisper. The boy responded only by contorting his face as he neared Inaya.

"Do you have a pass?" Raymond said, his voice loud and authoritative.

Inaya sensed the ambassador wanted her to know he didn't agree with the student's snide remark. But she was only slightly appeased. She wanted to shrink through the floor right then.

The girl's nose flared in irritation as she flashed a yellow slip of paper in front of Raymond then rolled her eyes in exaggerated annoyance.

"If you want to keep the school safe," the boy said, a look of disgust on his face as he glanced at Inaya, pulling his girlfriend closer to him, "then worry about that terrorist you're escorting."

The girl snickered.

"You wouldn't want to be party to killing innocent students."

Inaya's eyes widened in shock and embarrassment, but the boy and girl had already turned away.

Raymond stood still, his eyes fiery as he stared after them, their laughter still audible as they disappeared down the hall.

"Idiots," he muttered to himself.

His lips formed a thin line as he looked at Inaya. "I'm sorry about that," he said with a sigh. "Unfortunately, only the student ambassadors went through multicultural sensitivity training."

Inaya huffed as she walked away from the amabassor toward the hall leading to the front office. *And I'm still a fundamentalist to you.*

***

Still shaken, Inaya was silent as she rode in the back of the car after her parents finished the registration process. Her face was warm in shame and upset. She sunk low into her seat until the car was far from the school. She couldn't shake the feeling of shame she felt right then. Even her mother and stepfather looked like extremists.

A wave of embarrassment passed through Inaya as she wondered what Raymond must think of her. *Ugh.* Why did he have to be standing in the hall when her parents walked out of the office?

She couldn't imagine what Raymond thought of her stepfather's obvious Arab appearance and large beard—and her mother's all-black Saudi-style abaya and face veil.

*"But I'm not a fundamentalist."*

Oh really?

That was probably the question Raymond had been too polite to ask.

And so what? Inaya thought to herself. She couldn't care less what that stupid so-called student ambassador thought of her.

Multicultural sensitivity? Yeah right. Raymond's charade of kindness was only because he was on hall duty. He probably wouldn't want to be seen talking to the Arab-sounding girl outside of that.

Inaya felt sick as the sound of Arabic came from the car speakers. She rolled her eyes. A "fundamentalist lecture." That's probably what Raymond would think of this Arab sheikh's guttural exhortations.

*"Cool. Do you speak Arabic?"*

A knot loosened in her chest at the memory, but Inaya didn't trust the softness she felt toward Raymond right then. After all, he wasn't on her side.

*"Then worry about that terrorist you're escorting."*

Inaya's head throbbed, and she slumped in her seat.

*"I look forward to having a normal life again."*

What? Had Inaya really said that to her friends?

Right then, Inaya had no idea what "normal" even meant…and it frustrated her that, as a Muslim girl, she'd be denied any opportunity to learn.

# 4

## Qur'an Class

"Oh, I can't tell you how excited we are to have Inaya with us." The woman's green eyes sparkled as she stood next to the teacher's desk Saturday morning. "We've heard so much about her."

Inaya forced a smile and glanced around at the walls of the small classroom. White papers bearing large, black-outlined Arabic letters filled with children's colored scribbles were taped to the walls. For a second, Inaya forgot she was at the Muslim school that was a forty-minute drive from her family's apartment. She felt like she was in Saudi Arabia right then. Inaya looked away and concentrated on staring at her shoes.

"How long did it take you to memorize Qur'an?"

An inscription carved into a student's desk caught Inaya's eye and she lifted her head to make out what it said. She ran the tips of her fingers over the carving.

"Inaya." Veronica's voice was of forced politeness, the tone Veronica used in public when she was annoyed with her daughter.

Blinking in confusion, Inaya turned to her mother.

"Sister Amal is talking to you."

Inaya smiled her apology, realizing that the question could only have been meant for her. Her mother hadn't memorized Qur'an yet.

"Three years," Inaya said, forcing a smile as she studied Sister Amal for the first time.

Inaya wondered if her mother would let her wear a pink hijab, white blouse, and embroidered skirt instead of the black hijab and *jilbaab* she'd worn in Saudi Arabia. Sister Amal's outfit was one Inaya could stomach wearing to school.

Would Inaya wear the same outfit every day? During her entire first week of school, the only indication that she had even bothered to change clothes had been the different color trims on the edge of her head cover and sleeves. But she doubted anyone had even noticed.

"Is she some sort of Goth or something?" one student had whispered during Biology class. "Looks more like an Arab Emo to me," the other had responded sarcastically.

"*MaashaAllah*," Amal said, tilting her head to the side as she smiled at Inaya. "You're such an inspiration. I hope you'll agree to work at the weekend school."

Inaya felt the beginning of a headache, but she forced a smile, stopping short of consenting. She didn't know anyone here. How could she just walk in and start teaching, even if the students would be children?

"She would love to," Veronica said as she put an arm around Inaya's shoulders and pulled her close, grinning proudly at her daughter. "She taught Qur'an in Saudi Arabia."

"Really?" Amal's eyes widened, and she couldn't contain her excitement. "That's wonderful, *maashaAllah*."

Amal shook her head and sighed, her expression still pleasant. "You have no idea how hard it is for us to keep a Qur'an teacher. We've only been open for three weeks, and already they've had two teachers."

Amal's face registered concern as she looked at Inaya. "Do you mind teaching a class for us?"

Inaya glanced uncertainly at her mother, whose smile told her that she didn't have much of a choice. Inaya gave Amal a tight-lipped smile. "Sure," she said. "When do I start?"

Amal smiled apologetically and glanced at the clock on the wall behind them, and Inaya's chest constricted in anxiety. "The students should be here in fifteen minutes."

***

When the last of the eighteen children settled into their seats, Inaya's heart hammered in her chest. She parted her lips to speak, but she found difficulty catching her breath.

Before Inaya could introduce herself, two boys hopped from their seats and began wrestling each other. Some boys and girls twisted their bodies to watch.

Two students in the front row, a boy and a girl, stared at Inaya unblinking, jaws agape, as if trying to figure out where she had come from.

A little girl raised her hand anxiously, squirming in her seat as she tried to get Inaya's attention.

A sharp pain knotted at Inaya's temples, and she glanced at the clock. How would she last fifty-four more minutes? In Riyadh, all of her teaching had been in her home with peers. She had no idea how to handle a real class.

The little girl began bobbing up and down in her chair and waving a hand back and forth. "Teacher! Teacher! Teacher!"

Because Inaya had no idea what else to do, she pointed to the girl and nodded.

"Is Sister Zaynab coming back?"

Inaya creased her forehead. She didn't even know who Sister Zaynab was. "I…don't know."

"Will you be our new teacher?"

"Well…yes, I think so."

Suddenly, the commotion of the wrestling match quieted, and one of the boys who had been fighting glared at Inaya, an angry pout on his face. "We don't want you to teach us. You look stupid."

"*You* look stupid," the other boy said as he shoved his opponent in an apparent attempt to resume the fight.

Inaya's face burned in shame, and she felt anger building in her chest. "Sit down! Now!"

Commotion broke out immediately, as if Inaya's yelling had given the students permission to become rowdy themselves. Some students got out of their seats to watch the fight. Others wandered around the classroom observing the modest decorations on the walls. Still others stared with unabashed amazement at the new teacher.

How dare these children disrespect her! She might not be a real teacher, but she was much older than these five-, six-, and seven-year-olds.

"I *said*..." Inaya raised her voice until her throat hurt. "...sit down! *Now!*"

A hush of silence rippled through the room until the children stared at Inaya in disbelief. The boys who had been fighting scrambled to their feet, their breathing audible as they glowered at Inaya.

The girl who had asked the question shrank in her seat, her eyes wide in fear. "You don't have to yell at us," she muttered, her voice shaky.

Inaya's head pounded and her hands trembled in nervousness. "Sit down," she said in a calmer tone, her eyes raking the classroom. "Please."

Inaya drew in a deep breath as the children took their seats, their expressions uneasy. She reached for the large Qur'an on the teacher's desk and lifted the heavy book as she slid into the wooden chair.

"Now," she said, uncertain what she should do next, her eyes jumping nervously from the Qur'an to the class, "let's recite *Al-Faatihah*."

\*\*\*

"What?" Kayla wrinkled her nose from where she sat on her bed across from Inaya. "Is that like Bible study or something?"

Inaya sighed as she leaned back on the palms of her hands, her legs folded like a pretzel in front of her. It was Saturday afternoon, and Veronica had gone out with Kayla's parents. Inaya's gaze shifted momentarily to Abdullah, who slept in his car seat on the floor of the bedroom.

Inaya shrugged. "Yeah, I guess so."

"That's messed up." Kayla leaned against the headboard and tilted her head to the side to continue twisting her hair. "I can barely stand babysitting. I can't imagine teaching."

Inaya exhaled audibly. "Yeah, I know."

There was a pregnant pause, and Inaya felt Kayla staring at her.

"Are you going to wear those Arab clothes to school every day?"

It took a moment for Inaya to register her cousin's question. Inaya creased her forehead and sat up, her hands now in her lap. "What?"

"Those black robes." Kayla gestured her head toward the chair where Inaya's *khimaar* and *jilbaab* hung over its back. "Will you wear them to school?"

Inaya contorted her face in offense. "Yes."

"Chill," Kayla said, her lip upturned. "I was just curious."

Inaya rolled her eyes. What was Kayla getting at? That Inaya's clothes were ugly or something? Kayla saw Inaya every day at school. They even had English class together. So Kayla knew that Inaya would wear the clothes to school because Inaya had already worn them to school—every day.

"I just don't get it, that's all."

"Get what?" Inaya glared at Kayla defensively.

"Why you dress like that."

"I'm Muslim, Kayla. Quit trying to act stupid."

Kayla narrowed her eyes at her cousin. "Girl, what's your problem? I didn't know Muslims had to dress like somebody died."

Inaya widened her eyes, wounded. "I'm not dressing like somebody died. I'm dressing like a Muslim."

"Then why doesn't Nasra dress like you?"

Inaya grew quiet. Nasra was a senior at the school and was well-liked despite being openly Muslim, at least that's the impression Inaya got.

Inaya had met Nasra on Thursday during lunch period when Nasra had come to the table where Inaya was sitting with Kayla and her friends. After handing them a flyer about her campaign for Student Council, Nasra shared what she planned to do if she were elected president.

But Inaya remembered nothing of what Nasra had said. Inaya couldn't get over how Nasra spoke to her classmates as if she were their equal, as if she wasn't wearing a cloth draped around her head and neck and an oversized shirt that hung to the knees of her baggy jeans. Nasra had even given Inaya salaams before she left to the next lunch table.

But Inaya had averted her gaze and mumbled a reply, fearing her schoolmates would overhear and think she was weird for speaking a foreign language.

"Nasra is different," Inaya said, her voice tight with emotion. She hoped her cousin would change the subject.

Kayla squinted her eyes curiously. "But aren't you both Muslim?"

Inaya had no idea what to say. "Yeah, but…" But what?

"Why don't you just dress like Nasra?" Kayla said. "Then you wouldn't look so drab."

Inaya groaned and rolled her eyes.

Abdullah started to squirm and whine in his car seat.

"No offense," Kayla said.

"Just forget it," Inaya said as she shoved herself off the bed and kneeled next to her little brother. "It doesn't matter anyway."

But it did matter, Inaya thought. The deadweight of dread hung in her chest as she rocked her little brother's chair back and forth to quiet his cries. She had no idea how she would stomach walking into school Monday morning wearing the same "drab" black *khimaar* and *jilbaab* she had worn all last week.

*"Is she some sort of Goth or something?"*

Inaya winced at the thought.

Why did she have to look like some Gothic freak? What was wrong with wearing bright colors and baggy pants?

Abdullah's cries grew louder and Inaya gripped the edge of her brother's chair and rocked it more urgently.

"Do you need some help?"

Inaya turned to see Kayla standing behind her. "Yes, I do," Inaya said with a sigh of frustration. "Please."

# 5

## The Late Pass

Monday morning, Inaya sat looking out the passenger-side window next to Kayla, who was giving her a ride to school. Inaya felt uncomfortable in her drab all-black garb, but a surge of nervous excitement sent her heart racing as she glanced down at the sliver of jean skirt peeking through the open buttons of her *jilbaab*.

The idea had come to her Sunday afternoon, and Inaya had trembled at its simplicity. Why was she stressing over wearing the same thing every day when all she had to do was wear something different? If her mother wanted her to wear all black, she would—until she got to school.

It wasn't like she wouldn't be covered, Inaya told herself, quieting the guilt that twisted a knot of anxiety in her chest. She just wouldn't wear the *jilbaab*. Other Muslim girls wore loose, modest clothes in place of the bulky over-garment that was favored in Saudi Arabia. Did that make them bad Muslims? They still wore hijab.

"Who will you vote for for Student Council?"

It took a few seconds for Inaya to register Kayla's question. Inaya creased her forehead and turned to her cousin.

"I don't know," she said, her voice even despite her pounding heart.

The mention of Student Council reminded Inaya of the large sign she had seen posted just beyond the entrance to the school on Friday afternoon.

*Raymond Dirks for Student Council President. He'll get the job done. Period.*

Inaya had halted her steps as the student ambassador's motionless eyes held her gaze from the large smiling picture affixed to the poster stand. Her heart grew warm in flattery at knowing this candidate personally, and she smiled to herself.

"Doesn't he look good?" The question had seemed to come out of nowhere as Inaya stood in the hall. Startled, Inaya had spun on her heels to find herself staring into the face of the very person she was admiring in the photo.

Raymond had laughed then patted her on the shoulder, apparently forgetting the lessons from his multicultural sensitivity training.

"Vote for me, okay?" he said with a wink before disappearing down the hall to distribute the paper flyers he had tucked under an arm.

"I think I'm going for Nasra," Kayla said.

As Kayla steered the car into the parking lot of the school, Inaya could still feel the impression of Raymond's hand on her shoulder, and her face grew warm in nervous excitement.

Inaya just wished her *khimaar* was another color, but all her head covers were black. She hoped the black scarf wouldn't look too awkward with her white pearl-button shirt and long blue-jean skirt. Her slip-on shoes were black, so maybe the black hijab would actually complement her outfit today.

The buzz of chatter and commotion was intoxicating as Inaya pulled open one of the heavy double doors leading to the school. Inaya held the door and stepped aside until Kayla entered then followed her cousin inside.

"Why don't you vote for Raymond?" Inaya asked as she fell in step next to Kayla. They were making their way to the girls' bathroom to check their appearances as they did each morning.

Kayla shrugged. "I just think Nasra would do a better job."

Inaya nodded as if considering her cousin's comment, but her thoughts were on removing the black garment as quickly as she could. Besides, she didn't want to think of Nasra right then. For some reason, the girl made Inaya uncomfortable.

Inaya yanked at the fabric of her *jilbaab* and began unfastening the buttons as she and her cousin neared the end of the hall.

"Anyway," Kayla said, pushing open the door to the girls bathroom, "Raymond gets picked for everything. I think it's time somebody else got a chance."

"He was president before?" Inaya asked absently. Her heart raced wildly as she shrugged off the *jilbaab* and walked toward the full-size mirror, where a few students were applying make-up.

"No," Kayla said as she ran a hand over her fresh twists. "But he was vice president for two years in a row."

Inaya balled up the garment and stuffed it into her book bag. "I like Raymond," she said, shocked by her own boldness. "I mean, as president of Student Council," she said too quickly, her eyes darting to Kayla anxiously.

Kayla snorted, a smile teasing one side of her mouth. "Who doesn't?" She rolled her eyes. "I don't think the boy has a single flaw."

Inaya felt possessive of Raymond all of a sudden. Did Kayla like him or something? Inaya scolded herself at the thought. Even if Kayla did, so what? Inaya was Muslim—and plain-looking. No one as handsome and popular as Raymond would even notice her.

But the girl who stared back at Inaya in the mirror startled her. Inaya's appearance was in stark contrast to her growing insecurity. The white blouse and skirt fell loosely over Inaya's form but accented her shape so attractively that it was breathtaking.

*Is that me?*

Inaya's body jerked as someone yanked on her arm, the motion causing the *khimaar* to loosen itself from Inaya's head.

"You go girl!" Kayla said, a wide grin on her face. She squeezed Inaya's arm approvingly as she looked Inaya up and down. "That really suits you."

Inaya smiled despite herself as she reached up to readjust her hijab. "You think so?"

Kayla nodded emphatically. "Definitely."

Inaya was still smiling as she tucked a piece of black fabric under her chin, but the *khimaar* did not stay in place. Groaning, Inaya pulled the cloth from her head then carefully set it back on her head. A few braids escaped from the elastic ponytail holder, making it impossible to readjust the head cover without re-securing the elastic band. Inaya sighed and draped the cloth over her shoulders so she could fix her hair.

"I'm glad you gave up that—"

The shrilling of the bell interrupted Kayla midsentence, and her eyes widened in fear. "Oh my God," Kayla said. The other students scrambled out the bathroom, shoving roughly past Kayla and Inaya. "That's the second bell."

Inaya's heart raced as she fumbled with the band at the back of her head. She didn't want to be late, but if she didn't leave now with Kayla, she probably would be. Inaya was still learning her way around the large school, and she doubted she could find her class on her own.

"Come on." Kayla's eyes pleaded, annoyance on her face. "We only have a minute before they give late passes."

Inaya quickly tucked her braids into a small bun then reached for the *khimaar* that was draped over her shoulders. When she didn't feel the cloth immediately, she looked down at herself then at her reflection. The fabric was nowhere in sight.

"What?" Kayla's voice became concerned all of a sudden.

"My hijab—" Frantic, Inaya patted herself and looked at her reflection again.

"Your *what*?"

"M-m-my..." Inaya was so panicked she couldn't speak. A hand went to her head as her eyes scanned the floor near where she stood.

It took Kayla only a second to register what her cousin was looking for, and she too turned and started to look for the cloth.

"Can't you just find it later?"

A surge of anger rose in Inaya's chest, and she started to respond flippantly. But her thoughts were interrupted as she saw a flash of black peeking from behind the wall leading to the restroom exit.

Inaya rushed toward it, but she withdrew her hand and halted her steps when she saw that the *khimaar* was trampled with shoeprints and lay next to an overflowing trashcan. A small puddle of dirty water glistened from beneath the fabric, and a discarded paper towel lay crumpled atop.

"There it is," Kayla said, sighing in relief as she grabbed the *khimaar* from the floor and shoved it into Inaya's hand. "Now let's go."

Kayla pulled Inaya by the arm, and Inaya shuffled her feet as she reluctantly followed her cousin.

Inaya felt naked beneath the bright fluorescent lights of the wide hallway as Kayla quickened her steps and let go of Inaya's arm. Inaya fell back and dragged her feet, letting the gap between her and her cousin grow wider.

"Your class is right around the corner upstairs," Kayla called out over her shoulder.

"See you at lunch," Kayla said before she broke into a sprint toward her own classroom.

But Inaya's thoughts were not on being late to class. As she slowly approached the staircase, her eyes were on the soiled *khimaar* balled up in her hand.

She needed to put on her hijab. The urgency of the thought made Inaya glance back at the bathroom as she mentally calculated how long it would take to clean the cloth and put it back on.

Maybe she should just skip homeroom, she considered. That way she'd have time to get properly dressed.

But the cold dampness of the fabric repulsed her. Could she really put the filthy cloth back on her head, even if she washed it in the sink first?

"Get to class!" someone called out from down the hall.

The voice reminded Inaya of Raymond, and a strange sensation came over her. She glanced behind her, anxious to see if Raymond was on hall duty.

Inaya felt disappointed when she saw that it was only a teacher.

The teacher glowered at Inaya as the late bell rang, and Inaya quickened her steps as she yanked at the zipper of her backpack and stuffed the cloth inside.

\*\*\*

Inaya felt invisible as she stood waiting for a late pass in the front office. The secretary did not even look up as she set the late-student roster in front of Inaya. Inaya furrowed her brows as she lifted the pen attached to a clipboard and leaned forward to write her name. Inaya's eyes danced between the roster and the secretary as Inaya scribbled her name and slid the clipboard back to the woman.

"Your student I.D. please," the secretary said, no trace of forced politeness in her tone. But when Inaya had come to retrieve her class schedule the week before, the same woman had raked her eyes over Inaya with such scrutiny that Inaya had felt suffocated in her skin.

"My I.D.?" Inaya creased her forehead as she looked over the desk at the secretary, who held out a hand and wore a courteous smile that Inaya had imagined was reserved for other students.

"Your student identification card, dear."

"Oh… I don't have one."

The woman knitted her eyebrows as she withdrew her hand and scribbled an illegible note next to Inaya's name. "All students must carry an identification card on school premises."

"I'm sorry," Inaya said. "I didn't know."

The secretary frowned, but her expression remained pleasant. "Who's your homeroom teacher?"

Inaya creased her forehead. "Mr. Rhodes," Inaya said finally. She was still trying to remember her teachers' names.

The woman removed a pen from a canister and wrote a note on a yellow sticky note then handed it to Inaya.

"Give this to Mr. Rhodes," the secretary said. "You'll need to get your I.D. form from him. Make sure it's signed, then take it to the Student Affairs Office.

Inaya accepted the small note, but her expression was blank as she looked at the secretary. "Where's that?"

"Next to the gymnasium on the first floor," the woman said. "That's where you'll get your I.D."

Inaya nodded and started for the door.

"Don't forget this."

Inaya turned to find the secretary smiling, her hand outstretched holding a late pass.

Inaya smiled gratefully. "Thank you."

Ten minutes later, Inaya was carrying the signed I.D. form and her late pass as she descended a flight of steps. A surge of excitement shot through her, and her hands trembled. If she took her I.D. picture now, she would be forever invisible—an anonymous, bareheaded nobody—just as she had been before her mother accepted Islam.

*Inaya Donald.* That's what her I.D. card would read just below her headshot.

*Thank God for Chris Donald*, Inaya thought. Without the headscarf and over-garment, her father's "normal" family name could work in her favor. No one would mistake her for Arab anymore—or Muslim.

But Inaya's confidence waned as she approached the doorplate that read "Student Affairs Office."

What was she doing? Was she out of her mind?

For a moment, Inaya's legs felt as if they would give out. She halted her steps to lean against a wall, the throbbing in her head making her feel dizzy.

What if her mother found out? Or even her stepfather?

*Thanks for teaching us…love for Allah's sake.*
*Thanks for telling us to pray and cover—*
*Without taking a break!*

Inaya could almost hear Rafa and her friends reciting the poem, their words an eerie taunt that traveled across a continent and an ocean to haunt Inaya at this moment.

Inaya dropped her head in shame and felt the deadweight of the black cloth that was stuffed into the bag slung over her shoulder.

Why didn't Inaya just wash it in the restroom and dry it with the automatic hand dryer?

"May I help you?"

Inaya jerked her shoulders in surprise and stood up straight. She hadn't heard the door open.

Arms folded authoritatively, a middle-aged woman with gray streaks in her hair stood in front of the now-open door to the Student Affairs Office. For some reason, the woman reminded Inaya of her grandmother.

"A *Muslim*?" Inaya's grandmother had said the day she learned that her success-driven, stunningly beautiful, only daughter had left the church. She had nearly spat the words, but even if Veronica's mother had said nothing, her disgust was unmistakable in her expression of exaggerated confusion and disapproval.

Similarly, this woman's rich brown face was contorted so violently that Inaya shuddered—just as Inaya had before her grandmother so many years before.

"I'm sorry, I…" Inaya muttered. Her throat went dry and she quickly handed the lady the signed student identification form that her homeroom teacher had given her. Inaya coughed and cleared her throat. "…I just need an I.D."

The woman snatched the paper and glowered at Inaya suspiciously before slowly taking her eyes from Inaya to review the form.

Inaya's heart raced as the expression of disapproval became more pronounced as the woman skimmed the form.

"You should've just come in," the lady said finally, her voice raspy. She lifted the form in the air and waved Inaya inside.

The smell of cigarettes and stale coffee burned Inaya's nostrils as she followed the woman inside. As the woman closed the door behind them, Inaya felt suffocated in the cramped space. She glanced around for a place to sit.

"Put your bag over there." The woman nodded her head toward a floor-to-ceiling, industrial-style metal shelf that lined the entire right wall and was filled with stacks of bulging file folders.

Reluctantly, Inaya took a step toward the messy array of files and saw that there were more files stacked on the floor. Inaya scanned the area until she found an empty space between the large wooden desk and the metal shelves. She dropped her bag there then stood uncertainly next to the only chair she saw other than the large leather one behind the desk.

"Please take a seat," the woman said, her voice exhausted and irritated. She slammed the identification form on the desk as she sat down then pulled her chair closer. "I have a lot of work to do."

Inaya quickly sat down and folded her hands neatly on her lap, sitting up straight.

"I'm Mrs. Ford." The woman reached for a coffee mug and brought it to her mouth and took a sip. Still holding the glass cup, Mrs. Ford eagerly read the rest of the I.D. form that Inaya had handed her. "I presume you're new to this school?"

Inaya felt Mrs. Ford's eyes on her and she nodded nervously, her mind on the *khimaar* stuffed in the backpack that was now out of reach. "Yes, I am."

"Then you need to know that you are not allowed on the premises without a school-issued picture I.D.," Mrs. Ford said tartly.

Inaya nodded, her face growing warm at the word *picture.* Was she really going through with this? Maybe she should get her hijab. Her eyes darted toward where her book bag lay next to a pile of file folders.

"Go through that divider." Mrs. Ford stood and nodded her head toward a curtain to the left. She took a sip of coffee and glanced at the I.D. form again, sending Inaya's heart racing at what was about to happen.

"You'll see a wooden stool," Mrs. Ford said as she set down the coffee mug and leaned forward to pick up a pen. "Sit there and wait for me."

Inaya nodded and stood, hesitating as she glanced back at her book bag.

After scribbling something on the form, Mrs. Ford set the pen back down and started toward the divider herself.

Heart racing, Inaya quickened her steps and moved the thick curtain aside as she stepped into the photo studio. The room was murky and dark except for the sliver of light spilling from Mrs. Ford's office.

Inaya looked around for a light switch, but the click of Mrs. Ford's shoes stopped her. Inaya walked quickly toward the silhouette of a barstool and slid onto the chair a second before Mrs. Ford yanked open the curtain and stepped inside herself.

There was a popping and buzzing sound, and bright light spilled in Inaya's direction, making her face burn uncomfortably. She heard the sound of the curtain being yanked closed, but she didn't look in the direction of the sound.

Inaya was settled on the student I.D. chair now, and she had no choice but to take her school picture.

Anyway, it wasn't her fault that the *khimaar* was completely ruined.

And even if it were, there was nothing Inaya could do about it now.

# 6

## The Gift

"Can you believe he asked me to stop wearing *niqaab*?"
Veronica's angry voice carried to the living room as Inaya
stepped inside the apartment Monday afternoon.

"I know," Veronica said, her voice slightly muffled as
Inaya quietly closed the front door and locked it. "That's
what I was worried about when I married an Arab. They're
so weak in their religion. *Astaghfirullah*."

Upon realizing she was alone, Inaya yanked the damp
*khimaar* from her head and shrugged off the wrinkled
*jilbaab* that she hadn't bothered to button. After a day of
walking bareheaded through the halls (and enjoying it),
Inaya had hand-washed the head cover in a restroom sink
before going home.

"What about Inaya?" Veronica said, the question halting
Inaya's steps toward her mother's room to give salaams. "If
I take off my face veil, how do I explain that to her?"

Veronica groaned. "Next thing you know, he's going to
ask me to start wearing colored hijabs."

Silence followed for several seconds before Inaya heard
her mother moan in exhaustion. "I know, *ukhti*," Veronica
said. "I'm not saying it's *haraam*. I'm just scared he might
ask me to take off hijab eventually."

Inaya dragged herself to the kitchen, sadness weighing
on her as she thought of her father. She wondered when her
mother would take her to see him.

"I'm not overreacting," Veronica said defensively.
"Why should I uncover my face? Even if *niqaab*'s not
obligatory, what's the point of taking it off? I fear Allah, not
the people."

Inaya glanced at the clock. It was almost four o'clock, and she hadn't even prayed *Dhuhr*, the early afternoon prayer, and it was almost time for *Asr*.

"Because that stupid Arab culture made Sa'ad ashamed of his wife." Veronica's tone was indignant. "And now *I'm* supposed to feel ashamed for practicing the *Sunnah*?" She huffed. "They can keep their on-off hijab crap to themselves."

Inaya hurried to the bathroom in the hall and closed the door, shutting out her mother's conversation.

"*Bismillaah*," Inaya whispered, marking the start of her pre-prayer ablution. Inaya reached over the sink bowl and turned both knobs, releasing a thin stream of water into an upturned palm.

But even after mentioning Allah's name, anxiety still knotted in her chest, and she felt the beginning of a migraine.

Had she really spent the entire day without hijab?

Inaya rubbed the water on both hands then filled a hand with water before bringing it to her nose and mouth. The pounding in her head made it difficult to keep track of the steps of *wudhoo'*, but she squinted her eyes in concentration.

*Wash your right arm three times. Wudhoo! Wudhoo! Wash your left arm three times. Wudhoo! Wudhoo!* The rhythmic chant that Veronica had sung and clapped with her nine-year-old daughter came back to Inaya right then. At the time, Islam was still new and confounding to Inaya, but she recalled enjoying "playing in the sink" before prayer each day. It was like being baptized over and over again.

As a child, Inaya had prayed to "Allah" by following her mother's strange bowing and by muttering gibberish in an effort to imitate the foreign words her mother stumbled over. But Inaya never felt she got it right.

Veronica had told her daughter that God wasn't Prophet Jesus, and Inaya thought, *Okay, that makes sense.* But how could Inaya pray to a God she couldn't see? What was she supposed to think about if she couldn't imagine "Allah" in real form?

The Unseen Creator that Veronica spoke of was the same God that Inaya had imagined when she said "The Father." Why then was it so difficult for Inaya to erase from her mind the image of a white-haired man with long hair and a flowing beard?

After seven years of being Muslim, things were not as befuddled in Inaya's mind, but there was still that lingering feeling that something was missing. It was as if her mother took off in a sprint and had grabbed Inaya's hand and dragged Inaya along before Inaya knew where they were going. Inaya had felt that her legs were too weak and her breath too short as her energy steadily waned.

Then one day her mother snatched Daddy away too.

Inaya turned the faucet knobs, and the stream of water disappeared as the bathroom grew suddenly quiet. In the mirror above the sink, a sad girl stared back at Inaya.

Still, at sixteen years old, Inaya found that no motions of the Muslim prayer and no talks of an Unseen God—or even her mother's promise of everlasting bliss "one day"— helped Inaya make sense of Daddy being snatched from their lives.

*"Pretty brown eyes,"* Chris used to sing to Inaya, *"you know how much I love you."*

Inaya averted her gaze from her reflection. Why couldn't Inaya have done something to make her father stay?

*No, Daddy, don't go. Don't go!*

Such simple words, a simple protest.

But Inaya had sat mute, a frozen smile on her face. She said nothing as her father kneeled in front of her and brushed her forehead with a kiss.

"It's okay, Pretty Brown Eyes," he'd said as he wiped her eyes. But Inaya hadn't even known she was crying.

"You're Daddy's gift." He pinched her cheek playfully, but Inaya remembered how sad his eyes had looked that day.

"Is that you, Inaya?" Veronica called out as Inaya opened the bathroom door and stepped into the hall. A second later, Veronica stood opposite Inaya, Abdullah resting his head on his mother's shoulder as she patted him rhythmically on the back.

*You know how much I love you.* The song Inaya's father had sang to her was in his eyes when he'd said goodbye, and even now it made Inaya's throat close in sadness.

Inaya forced a smile as she met her mother's gaze and closed the bathroom door. "*As-salaamu'alaikum,*" Inaya said, offering the Muslim greeting of peace.

"*Wa'alaiku-mus-salaam,*" Veronica replied, a tired smile on her face.

In the awkward silence that followed, Inaya saw the question in her mother's eyes. She was wondering if Inaya had overheard any of the conversation.

"I didn't know you were home," Veronica said.

"I just got here," Inaya lied. "But I had to rush to the bathroom."

"*Alhamdulillaah.*" Veronica looked relieved as she praised God, and Inaya sensed that her mother was grateful that Inaya hadn't come home while she was talking to her friend.

Veronica drew Inaya into a half hug, and Inaya inhaled the scent of breast milk and baby powder.

"Did you pray *Dhuhr*?" Veronica asked after she released Inaya.

"I'm about to now."

"Good," Veronica said as she hurried back down the hall toward her room. "I'll pray with you," she said over her shoulder. "I lost track of time."

\*\*\*

47

The first thing that Inaya saw when she walked into her room after prayer was a large Macy's bag. Curious, Inaya walked to her bed and lifted it from the comforter before peering inside. There was an unwrapped gift box inside.

Inaya sat on the edge of her bed and carefully pulled out the box then set it on her lap. She held the sides of the top and shook it to release it from the bottom. Inside was a card with a picture of falling leaves on top of translucent white paper.

Inaya lifted the card and opened it. She recognized her stepfather's script immediately.

*Congratulations, Inaya. Your mother told me you're a Qur'an teacher now. Don't worry. First days are always tough.*

*You're a bright girl, maashaAllah. Just be yourself and the children will love you, bi'idhnillah.*

*Here's something I hope will make you feel better.*

*Love, Dad*

The word *Dad* made Inaya feel distant momentarily. She already had a father. Why did Sa'ad and Veronica imagine he could be replaced?

The sound of paper crumpling interrupted Inaya's thoughts as she removed the white paper and tossed it on her bed. There was the faint scent of new clothes as folded fuchsia cloth came into view.

Inaya set the box to the side and stood as she held the reddish-purple material in front of her.

A smile creased a corner of Inaya's mouth, and tears welled in her eyes. Maybe Sa'ad would never be "Dad" to her, but that didn't keep him from wedging a place for himself in her heart.

Inaya rushed to the mirror to try on the new *khimaar*. She would wear the hijab to Qur'an school every Saturday, she decided as she wrapped the cloth around her head. She tucked a corner under her chin and ran a palm over its softness. She liked how the color brought out her smooth complexion and brown eyes. She couldn't keep from smiling at her reflection.

Inaya thought of school the next morning, and her heart dropped. Did she have the strength to put her hijab back on?

Did she even want to?

# 7

# The Competition

"Sorry about yesterday," Kayla said Tuesday morning as she turned off the ignition and put the car in park. "I should've waited for you to get your head cover instead of rushing to class."

"It's okay." Inaya felt a sense of dread as she leaned forward to pick up the backpack she'd set at her feet. She didn't want to talk about hijab right then.

"No, really." Kayla frowned as she looked at her cousin. "I felt so bad when I saw you walking around without it." She sucked her teeth. "We could've washed it or something."

"Let's just forget it, okay?" Inaya pulled the door handle and shoved the car door open, swallowing the frustration building inside. She wished Kayla would shut up.

Kayla got out the car and pressed the button to lock the doors after they closed them. "I know you're probably pissed." She sighed. "But I'm really sorry."

Inaya dropped her book bag on the cement next to the car and tugged at the sleeves of her unbuttoned *jilbaab*. She slipped the garment off then kneeled to quickly unzip her bag and stuff the black bundle inside. She pulled a strap of her book bag over her shoulder as she stood.

Without the bulky over-garment, Inaya felt less constricted. The wide-legged jeans she wore were loose, but when she had gotten dressed that morning, she had trouble finding a shirt she liked. Now, the *khimaar* that her stepfather had bought covered her head and was draped low to conceal the bust of her fitting long-sleeve black shirt. But she still felt stifled. The fuchsia didn't match anything she wore.

"I like your new look, by the way," Kayla said with a smile.

Inaya grinned beside herself as she fell in step next to Kayla. "Thanks."

Inaya's heart pounded as she counted the steps to the bathroom. Inaya had already decided she would wear the *khimaar* to and from school—but not in the school building itself. She felt horrible about this decision, but she just couldn't imagine being taunted and stared at each day.

*Allah is Merciful,* Inaya told herself. *No sin is too great for Him to forgive.*

At least that's what her mother always said. Inaya didn't know if that was true, especially as far as her own soul was concerned. But it's what Inaya decided to believe. It was easier than thinking the alternative.

"Oh my God," Kayla said in the bathroom after Inaya removed her head cover. They were standing in front of the mirrors, and Inaya was stuffing the cloth into her bag. "Are you really taking all that off?"

Annoyed, Inaya rolled her eyes. "Yeah, so what?"

Kayla threw up her palms in defense. "Chill. I don't care what you do." She shrugged. "I'm just surprised, that's all."

"Why?" Inaya said defensively. "You're the one who said I looked like I'm going to a funeral."

Kayla chuckled at the reminder, but her face grew concerned a moment later.

"Are you sure this is a good idea?" Kayla spoke in a low whisper as she leaned toward Inaya in front of the large mirror. "Can't you get in trouble?"

Inaya responded by walking toward the bathroom exit. "Let's go," she said, her tone laced in irritation as she glanced over her shoulder to look at Kayla. "We're going to be late to homeroom."

In the hall, there the sudden sound of droves of students rushing to class, and a smirk tickled a corner of

Inaya's mouth. Bareheaded, Inaya was invisible, just another student going to class. The sense of empowerment this gave her was intoxicating, and laughter crawled in her throat. It felt so good to be normal.

"Hey, Kayla," a male voice called seconds after they emerged from the bathroom.

Kayla looked over her shoulder then broke into a grin. "Hey, Raymond!" she said with a wave, slowing her steps.

Inaya's face grew warm, and she turned to follow Kayla's gaze.

Raymond quickened his steps until he was next to Kayla. Inaya trembled in nervous excitement as she imagined how different—and attractive—she would look to the student ambassador. But her heart nearly stopped when she saw that he was holding someone's hand.

"Lyrica," Kayla said, a broad smile forming on her face. She pulled the girl into a hug, the girl still grasping Raymond's hand.

Inaya turned away as Raymond smiled fondly at Lyrica. But in that brief moment, Inaya had seen enough to make her feel insignificant.

Lyrica's rich brown skin glowed almost bronze, and her closely cropped hairstyle accented the model-like bone structure on her face. Lyrica stood at least three inches taller than Inaya and carried herself with a demeanor that exuded self-confidence and intelligence. A "Raymond Dirks for Student Council President" sticker was on her chest, drawing more attention to her attractive shape.

Inaya had to fight the urge to run back to the bathroom and put back on her *khimaar.*

"This is my cousin Inaya." Kayla stepped to the side and placed a hand on Inaya's shoulder.

"It's nice to meet you," Lyrica said, her wide smile brightening her face. She reached out to shake Inaya's hand. "I'm Lyrica, an old friend of Kayla's."

Inaya forced a smile as she accepted Lyrica's hand. She hoped she hadn't pulled her hand back too soon. She just couldn't stand the feel of the girl's soft palm and thin fingers that sported several silver bands.

"And I'm Raymond," the student ambassador said, reaching for Inaya's hand.

The formal introduction took her aback, and her face grew warm as their hands touched, her hand limply in his. For a moment she wondered if she was taking this "no hijab" choice too far.

"Nice to meet you again," Inaya said, a stiff smile on her face. She felt a burning urge for him to remember her right then.

He creased his forehead, his polite smile lingering. "You do look familiar…"

Kayla looked as if she wanted to say something, but Inaya hated her cousin for keeping quiet. Inaya didn't want the burden of reminding him. She was hoping he would remember without her help.

"We met last week," Inaya said with a confidence that sounded as if it belonged to someone else. "You thought I was Arab."

Raymond's face slowly registered recognition. "Oh…" The expression on his face was difficult for Inaya to read. "You're the Muslim from Saudi Arabia?"

A tinge of guilt pinched Inaya's chest. "Yes," Inaya said, maintaining a smile. "The fundamentalist," she added sarcastically.

Raymond laughed, and Inaya relaxed in that sound. He wasn't judging her after all.

"Well," he said, still smiling, "I didn't recognize you. You look…" His voice caught for a moment as he held her gaze, the admiration in his eyes sending Inaya's heart racing. "…different."

Inaya averted her gaze and waved a hand dismissively. "It's okay. I guess I don't recognize me either."

"You're Muslim?" Lyrica said, her eyes widening in pleasant surprise.

As she met Lyrica's gaze, Inaya felt a pang in her chest, and she knew at that moment, she would never like Lyrica, no matter how nice she might be.

"Yes," Inaya said in as even a tone as her annoyance would allow.

"That's awesome." Lyrica's eyes shined in sincerity. "I hope you don't mind if I bombard you with questions," Lyrica said with a laugh.

Lyrica grasped Raymond's hand as if it were the most natural thing in the world, and Inaya found herself hating Lyrica for taking Raymond for granted.

"That's fine," Inaya said, her strained smile fading.

"Good," Lyrica said as she smiled at Raymond briefly. "Because Raymond and I are completely fascinated by your religion."

Lyrica punched Raymond playfully with her free hand. "But don't let him near you unless I'm here." The words made Inaya stiffen, her lips twitching in an embarrassed smile. "I don't want him running off and finding God," Lyrica said. "It'll ruin our relationship."

"Women." Raymond shook his head, a pleasant expression on his face as he met Lyrica's gaze. "They're even jealous of religion."

"I didn't know Raymond was the religious type," Kayla said, her eyebrows rising. "I would've never guessed."

"Oh, he's not religious." Lyrica quickly brushed his cheek with a kiss. "I just want to keep it that way."

The sound of the bell ringing prompted Raymond and Lyrica to turn quickly and start down the hall, still holding hands.

"Inaya, it was nice meeting you," Lyrica shouted over her shoulder. She waved then blew a friendly kiss to Kayla, who did the same before rushing toward the staircase.

Groaning, Inaya shuffled behind Kayla, feeling completely uninspired to face the rest of the school day.

\*\*\*

"I think it's a toss-up," Raymond said from where he sat next to Lyrica at the lunch table with Kayla, Inaya, and two of Kayla's friends. He removed the plastic wrapping from the tuna sandwich he'd taken from a paper bag. "It's either Nasra or Lyrica this year."

Lyrica laughed with her lips closed as she swallowed the spoonful of pudding that she'd just put in her mouth. She waved the plastic spoon toward Raymond. "And why don't you think you'll win the Distinguished Student Award?" A smile played at her lips. "You won it your freshman year."

"That was three years ago," Raymond said, smiling affectionately at his girlfriend. "But I'm glad you haven't lost hope in me."

"They don't pick the same student twice," Kayla said before taking a sip of chocolate milk through a straw and looking toward Raymond. "It's like an unwritten teacher code or something."

Raymond and the other students chuckled, but Inaya only smiled. Her discomfort from earlier had loosened somewhat, but she still couldn't bring herself to participate in the conversation.

"It'll probably be Nasra," one of Kayla's friends said, boredom in her tone as she dipped a bundle of French fries in ketchup. "She's Arab and Muslim. It'll make the school look good."

"Oh, come on, Beth," Raymond said, his annoyed tone prompting Inaya to look in his direction. "I hate when people say stuff like that. It's like the only people who ever earn their awards are White Anglo-Saxon men."

"That's not what I meant, Raymond," Bethany said, her cheeks becoming flushed. "I'm just saying there's this whole media campaign to make people nice to Muslims. I'm tired of it."

Inaya winced. But she realized that, most likely, Bethany wasn't directing the comment at her. Bethany had met Inaya only once before, last week when Bethany had sat with Kayla for lunch. She probably didn't even recognize Inaya without hijab.

"Nasra is one of the smartest students in the school," Raymond said. "If she wins, it's because she deserved to, not because the school's trying to win Brownie points."

"But you can't deny that the school considers things like that," Lyrica said to Raymond. "Diversity influences their decisions."

"So what if it does?" Raymond said, frowning as he set down his partially-eaten sandwich. "That doesn't mean the person didn't deserve to win."

"Stop taking things so personally," Bethany said, rolling her eyes. "I wasn't talking about you."

"Me?" Raymond glared at her. "This has nothing to do with me."

"My point exactly." Bethany huffed. "Gosh, you're not even Muslim."

"But if what you say is true," Raymond said, "then you *would* be talking about me."

"I agree," Kayla's other friend said, sitting up. She turned to Bethany. "We can't call foul every time a non-White wins something. It's not fair."

Bethany slapped her hands on the table and stood. "I'm finished here." She picked up some plastic food containers she'd eaten from and tossed them onto the tray.

"This is exactly what I'm talking about," she said. "This whole country is turning into a bunch of bleeding-heart liberals. What happened to a good old-fashioned conversation?"

"What happened to good old-fashioned patience?" Kayla's friend said.

Bethany glowered at her friend before lifting the tray and walking away.

"Whew," Kayla said, laughing nervously once Bethany was out of earshot. "That was intense."

Raymond grumbled something under his breath and shook his head. Lyrica leaned toward him and put her arm around his shoulder as she whispered something in his ear.

For several seconds, an awkward silence stifled any attempt at conversation.

"Sorry about that," Kayla said.

When no one responded, Inaya looked up to find her cousin smiling apologetically at her.

Inaya creased her forehead. "Why are you sorry?"

Before Kayla could respond, Kayla's friend spoke. "Well, whoever wins the Distinguished Student Award," she said, "I'm happy for them. I don't think there's a higher award given at the school."

Kayla nodded and smiled. "Good luck, Lyrica," she said. "I think you deserve it."

At these words, Raymond's expression softened, and he grinned at his girlfriend. "I agree."

# 8

## Reunion

One Saturday evening in early October, Inaya sat staring out the passenger-side window as Sa'ad drove through the quiet streets of the townhouse community where Chris Donald lived. Though Inaya understood why her mother wasn't joining her on the visit, the knowledge did not erase the sadness Inaya felt at spending time with her father alone.

It was moments like these that Inaya found it difficult to understand why her mother's decision to accept Islam could not have included her father too. Inaya knew that it wasn't allowed for a Muslim woman to be married to a non-Muslim man, but why couldn't her mother have been more patient? Perhaps if Veronica had only given Chris more time, they could have remained married.

But it was always all or nothing with Veronica, Inaya thought sadly. Where Veronica saw black and white, Inaya and Chris saw gray. Even Sa'ad had advised Veronica to be more flexible in her practice of Islam. Of course, Sa'ad was not thinking of his wife's first marriage when he'd said this, but Inaya couldn't help thinking of his words right then.

"Just relax and enjoy yourself," Sa'ad said as he slowed the car in front of Chris's townhouse.

Inaya turned to see her stepfather smiling at her, his olive complexion distorted by the laugh lines next to his eyes. At his warm expression, Inaya's anxiety lessened. But she hadn't realized that she was stressed.

She smiled and nodded hesitantly. She wasn't so sure that relaxing was possible. But she would try to enjoy herself.

"I know all of this must be really confusing for you," Sa'ad said as he put the car in park.

Inaya met his gaze with her forehead creased.

"Becoming Muslim so young, your parents' divorce." He chuckled, but there was a trace of melancholy in that sound. "Then an Arab stepfather."

She averted her gaze. It was the first time Sa'ad had spoken so frankly with her. She didn't know what to say.

"I'm sorry, Inaya." The softness in his tone made her throat close. "I really am."

Inaya knew she should say something in response, but she couldn't find her voice.

"Just know if you need anything," he said, "I'm here."

She nodded, her gaze fixed on her folded hands.

"Thanks for the gift," she said, her voice barely above a whisper.

Sa'ad reached over and patted Inaya's hands. "You're welcome. I just wish I could give you something more. You deserve it, *maashaAllah*."

Inaya didn't feel as if she deserved anything, but she was grateful for the kind words.

"No," she said as she shook her head. "You deserve more." She hadn't meant to speak her thoughts aloud, but it was too late. She had never told Sa'ad she felt bad that she wasn't a good stepdaughter. She hated that she resented his presence when all he'd shown her was patience and kindness.

There was a pregnant pause.

Someone in the townhouse parted the curtains and peered outside.

"I better go," Inaya said.

"Call me when you're ready to come home."

Inaya nodded as she adjusted the strap of her purse over her shoulder. She pulled the passenger handle and pushed open the door.

"You look beautiful in that hijab, *maashaAllah*," Sa'ad said as Inaya stepped out the car.

The sides of Inaya's mouth creased in a smile. "You have good taste."

Sa'ad chuckled as Inaya shut the car door.

"*As-salaamu'alaikum*," Sa'ad called out.

Inaya waved to her stepfather before she made her way up the path leading to her father's home.

\*\*\*

"Inaya!" Chris said as Inaya stepped inside. He immediately pulled her into a hug, and Inaya inhaled the smell of coffee and spices. She remembered waking up as a child to find her father sitting reading the newspaper, a steaming coffee mug and a slice of freshly baked spiced bread on the kitchen table in front of him.

Chris released Inaya then held her face in his palms, a soft expression on his face. "You still have those pretty brown eyes."

Inaya grinned shyly and looked away, uncomfortable in the knowledge that along with her honey-colored skin, Inaya's brown eyes were a trait she inherited from her mother.

Music played from a stereo, the upbeat sound thumping in time with her heart, and Inaya recognized the song as R&B, the rhythm and blues some of her friends in Saudi Arabia liked to listen to.

"Come on in, sweetheart." Chris tugged on her hand, and Inaya followed him into the living room.

"How's your mother doing?" Chris asked as they settled on the couch. A tray of snacks and drinks was on the floor table in front of them.

For a fleeting moment, Inaya forgot that her parents were divorced. Years ago, the question was one her father would ask if Veronica was not feeling well.

"She's good." Inaya lifted her chin and loosed the fabric there then pulled the *khimaar* from her head.

"Do you like your new school?" He poured juice into a glass then handed it to Inaya. "Your uncle Anthony tells me you and Kayla are together."

"It's okay," Inaya said, setting the fuchsia hijab next to her before accepting the glass.

There was a brief pause as Chris poured himself some juice and Inaya sipped hers.

"Do the students treat you well?" he said. "As a Muslim, I mean."

She nodded. "Everybody's nice."

"I'm happy to hear that." He sighed, a slight smile on his face. "I was really worried about you."

Inaya smiled awkwardly, unsure what to say. Her gaze fell on the large clock on the wall, and it was then that she remembered the sunset prayer. She stood suddenly.

"Is there anywhere I can pray?" She hoped the abrupt change in subject did not offend her father.

"Of course," he said, standing immediately. "You can pray in my room."

Inaya held her fuchsia scarf in her hand as she followed him down the hall.

\*\*\*

"So if someone wants to become Muslim…" Chris said after Inaya rejoined him on the couch in the living room. His eyes were thoughtful, and it was then that Inaya remembered what Kayla had said.

*"You didn't know your dad is thinking about converting?"*

Inaya met her father's gaze curiously. Could it be that Kayla was not mistaken?

"…what do they need to do?"

Inaya reached for a packet of crackers and shrugged as she opened it. "They just need to say the *shahaadah*."

Chris squinted as if trying to recall something. He pointed to Inaya. "That's the testament of faith, right?"

"The testimony," she said with a nod.

"Hmm…" a thoughtful smile lingered on his face for some time.

"You want to become Muslim?" Inaya smirked. She was tempted to tease him about it, but something held her back.

He chuckled uncomfortably. "I can't say I want to…"

Inaya raised an eyebrow playfully. "Do you believe God is One?"

"I believed that all my life."

"Not part of the Trinity?"

"No." He shook his head. "I can't believe that. It doesn't make sense."

"So you don't believe God is Jesus or anything like that?"

His lips formed a thin line momentarily. "No, not anymore."

"Cool." Inaya grinned, unable to conceal her excitement.

Chris tossed his head back in laughter. "Cool?"

"Yeah." Inaya's eyes widened in excitement. "Now our whole family will be Muslim."

"Woe..." He put up a hand, laughter escaping his throat. "One step at a time."

"Daddy." Inaya grinned, an idea coming to her just then. "Why don't you do it now? Tonight, I mean."

He drew his eyebrows together. "Do what, sweetheart?"

"Say the *shahaadah*."

His eyes grew large, but a pleasant expression remained on his face. "I don't think I'm ready for that."

Inaya frowned. "Why not? Don't you believe in the Hereafter?"

"Of course."

"And that Islam is true?"

There was a thoughtful pause, but he nodded finally. "Yes, I do." His voice was somewhat subdued, his gaze distant.

"Then what are you waiting for?" Inaya smiled broadly, unable to contain her anxiousness.

Chris met his daughter's gaze, an amused expression in his eyes. "What if I'm not ready?"

Inaya contorted her face and chuckled. "That doesn't make any sense."

His eyebrows shot up, but there was humor in his eyes. "Oh, so you think this is just as easy as saying some words?"

She knitted her brows. "Yes..." Uncertainty clouded her expression. "Isn't it?"

Chris held Inaya's gaze briefly then shook his head. "If only it were."

She shook her head. "I don't understand."

Chris drew in a deep breath and exhaled. "If I become Muslim, my whole life has to change."

"Why?"

He furrowed his brows and looked at Inaya as if seeing his daughter for the first time. "Sweetheart..." His voice conveyed a desire to put his thoughts in simple terms.

Inaya leaned forward, her eyes intent, but her mind was a storm of confusion. Why did he think becoming Muslim wasn't as simple as testifying to the Oneness of God and belief in all His prophets?

Chris sighed. "Inaya, I have things I like to do. I…" He shook his head, apparently at a loss for words. "I have a fiancée. I have friends I've known since we were kids. I have a good job."

Inaya narrowed her eyes in an effort to understand, but she felt only a vague sense of comprehension. "But what does that have to do with becoming Muslim?"

"Everything." His eyes conveyed amazement at her lack of understanding. "Don't you realize what becoming Muslim would mean for someone like me?"

Inaya stared blankly at her father.

"I could lose Dana," Chris said. "I might be fired from my job. There'll be so many things I'll have to give up." He drew in a deep breath and exhaled. "And I'm not sure I'm ready for that."

Chris forced laughter. "I'm used to being looked at as normal, sweetheart," he said. "And as crazy as this may sound, I don't want that to change."

The word *normal* made Inaya think of her own desire to be invisible at school. It had even pushed her to remove her Islamic headdress.

Inaya averted her gaze, understanding her father's concerns but not wanting to.

"I know you're too young to understand all I'm saying," he said with a sigh. "But trust me. This isn't a simple decision. It'll mean sacrificing a lot more than I'm ready to."

Inaya wanted to tell him that she herself wasn't doing so well, but he spoke before she could say anything.

"Believe it or not," he said with a chuckle, "you're my inspiration." He smiled, his eyes on the ceiling briefly.

"When I see how strong you are," he said, "I'm so proud. And I think, 'That's my girl.'" He nodded. "And I tell myself, 'One day, I'll be like that.'"

An awkward smile formed on Inaya's face and she dropped her gaze to the crackers in her hand. She wondered what her father would think if he knew the truth.

# 9

## 𝒜 Second Chance

"I could do this all the time!" Lyrica threw her hands up and moved her body in rhythm to the music blaring from her iPod player on the schoolyard pavement.

Laughing, Kayla pushed herself off the grass and stood to join Lyrica. Kayla motioned to Inaya. "Come on," she said. "Let's dance."

It was a Wednesday afternoon and the three friends had decided to spend the lunch period outside. Though it was late October, the weather was comfortably cool, and they wore thin jackets.

Inaya felt the urge to join her friends, but she remained sitting on the grass, her knees pulled up in front of her as she thought about Raymond, who was at a Student Council meeting right then. A smile creased a corner of Inaya's mouth as she watched Lyrica sway back and forth, her attractive form difficult for Inaya to rip her eyes from.

"That's okay," Inaya said. "I'll just watch."

"Party pooper!" Lyrica called out.

Lyrica grasped Inaya's hands and pulled Inaya forward before she could protest. Laughing uncomfortably, Inaya stumbled to her feet, but she held back from dancing. She stood to the side, her arms folded loosely over her chest as she watched her friends.

"It's like I waited my whole life," Kayla sang along with the singer Chris Brown as she danced next to Lyrica, "for this one night."

Inaya nodded her head to the music, unable to calm the urge to join them.

"It's gon' be me, you, and the dance floor," Lyrica and Kayla sang out the chorus to "Forever."

Inaya moved her shoulders rhythmically and clapped her hands.

"Can I have this dance?"

Kayla and Lyrica looked toward Inaya and burst out laughing, and Inaya had the strange feeling that she was the butt of a joke.

She jerked in surprise when someone pulled her back by the shoulder. Her heart hammered in her chest when she turned to find Raymond smiling at her and taking her hand. Her face grew warm as he grasped both her hands.

She laughed uncomfortably as he moved their hands back and forth.

"Feels like we're on another level," Raymond sang.

Inaya was pleasantly surprised that he could carry a tune, and she moved in rhythm with him. But she kept a comfortable distance between her and him except for their joined hands.

Raymond winked at her as he continued singing. "…We can be two rebels, breaking the rules, me and you…"

At his last words, Inaya felt a surge of confidence swell in her chest and she danced more, unable to keep from laughing out loud, giddy in happiness. Next to them Lyrica and Kayla held hands and danced in step with each other.

Was Raymond just reciting the lyrics to a song, or did he really mean what he was saying?

A wave of hope swept through Inaya as flattery nestled in her chest. She found herself wishing Lyrica and Kayla were not next to them.

\*\*\*

"Why is the president of Student Council playing hooky?" Lyrica asked as she and Raymond walked hand-in-hand in front of Kayla and Inaya as they made their way back to the building for classes.

"It was a meeting," Raymond said, laughter in his voice, "not class."

"Oh, so you're shirking responsibility after you got our votes?" Kayla teased.

He glanced behind him, a smirk on his face. "You got it. I think it's time this school had a real politician."

They laughed and Inaya couldn't keep from laughing too.

"Nasra suggested we cut it short so we could eat," he said, his tone more serious. "I think I'm falling in love with the vice president."

Lyrica hit him on the head playfully.

At the mention of Nasra, anxiety constricted Inaya's chest.

It wasn't until last week that Nasra realized that Lyrica's and Raymond's "new friend" was the same girl she had seen in hijab over a month before. She had come to the lunch table to sit with Raymond to discuss some ideas for school clubs, and when she mentioned starting a Muslim Student Club, Raymond had suggested that Inaya could help Nasra.

The look on Nasra's face was a mixture of surprise and confusion, but she maintained a polite expression. "You're Muslim?"

"Yes," Inaya had said, her gaze absently falling to the tray of food that she was eating from.

"Oh…" That's when the look of recognition passed over Nasra's face, and Inaya wished Nasra would just leave the table. "Didn't you used to…"

Thankfully, Nasra had had the good sense not to finish the sentence, at least not verbally. But Inaya sensed the girl's harsh judgment concealed behind the kind expression.

"I'd love to have your help," Nasra said finally.

But Inaya grunted. "No thank you."

"Congratulations by the way," Kayla said as she fell in step next to Lyrica and Raymond after they entered the building, the iPod player bulky at Lyrica's side. "But I must admit," Kayla said, humor in her tone as she looked at Raymond, "I voted for Nasra."

Lyrica laughed. "Me, too."

"What?" Raymond looked genuinely shocked.

But Lyrica punched him playfully and winked. "Just kidding."

*** 

"You don't have to be such a jerk, you know."

Inaya turned to find Nasra, arms folded, smiling at her. School had ended twenty minutes before, and Inaya stood near the exit doors waiting for Kayla. She hadn't heard anyone come up behind her.

Students brushed past and hurried out the doors, and cool air rippled through Inaya's *jilbaab* each time the door opened. Inaya had slipped on the outer-garment as she stood in the hall. But she held her *khimaar* in her hand.

Inaya rolled her eyes and turned her attention back to the glass windows on the doors. "I don't know what you're talking about."

"You act like I bite."

Inaya clinched her teeth, but she did not meet Nasra's gaze. "Don't you have to go home or something?"

"Yes..." Nasra's tone held a hint of humor. "But my car isn't going anywhere without me."

Inaya huffed, but she didn't say anything.

"I'd really like you to help with MSC." Nasra's tone was softer, more serious.

"I don't want to help."

"We could really use you."

Inaya rolled her eyes. "Why? So you can secretly plan how to put me back on the right path?" Inaya turned to meet Nasra's gaze. "Is that why you're talking to me? You want to show me how nice you are? That you're open-minded so I can feel better when you start judging me?"

Nasra's expression remained pleasant, but Inaya detected a sense of sadness.

"No one's judging you," Nasra said.

"I saw the way you looked at me when you realized who I was." Inaya shook her head. "I'm not stupid."

Nasra sighed, and her eyes became reflective as she looked beyond Inaya out the rectangular window. "I know how you feel," she said. "Before I wore hijab, I used to think everyone was judging me too."

Inaya's eyes widened slightly. Nasra hadn't always worn hijab?

"I used to avoid hijabis and say they thought they were better than everybody else."

Inaya looked away.

"It took me a long time to accept that it wasn't the hijabis who were annoying me." Nasra put a hand on Inaya's shoulder. "I was just annoyed with myself."

There was a thoughtful pause as Inaya felt herself becoming irritated, but she didn't understand this feeling. She was glad when Nasra pulled her hand away.

"We could use you in the Muslim Student Club because it's obvious you're really smart and talented," Nasra said as she stepped forward to push the door open.

Nasra reached into her purse and pulled out a card. "This is my email, phone number, and Facebook I.D.," she said as she handed the card to Inaya. "Contact me if you change your mind."

\*\*\*

Inaya looked in the visor mirror as she wrapped the pink cloth around her head after Kayla had driven a safe distance from the school. Inaya secured a corner of the cloth under her chin then leaned back in her seat. Soft music wafted from the car speakers, and her thoughts grew distant as she looked out the passenger-side window.

"Raymond asked if he could have your phone number," Kayla said.

Inaya looked at her cousin, forehead creased. "What?"

"Raymond," Kayla repeated, glancing to her right to meet Inaya's gaze briefly. "I gave him your phone number. I hope that was okay."

Inaya's spirits lifted suddenly. She didn't know what to say. But the feeling of flattery passed as she realized that her mother or stepfather could answer the phone if Raymond called.

"You should've asked me first," Inaya said, betraying her true feelings. "I could get in trouble."

Kayla nodded, her thoughts elsewhere. "Sorry," she said, frowning. "I realized that after I gave it to him."

Inaya was silent as she listened to the melodious sound of music playing in the car. "Why didn't he ask me?"

"It was after lunch," Kayla said, "and he didn't know where to find you."

Inaya nodded absently, her gaze on the colored leaves of the passing trees.

"Did he say why?" Inaya said.

"I didn't ask," Kayla said, her tone subdued. "I didn't think it was my place."

Inaya's heart fluttered in hope, but Kayla's cautious tone made Inaya feel guilty. Was Inaya wrong to hope Raymond and Lyrica were having problems?

"Be careful," Kayla said after a thoughtful silence.

Inaya met her cousin's gaze, eyebrows drawn together. "Why?"

Kayla shrugged. "I'm worried about Lyrica, that's all."

*Whatever*, Inaya thought to herself.

"Let's just hope this is about his fascination with religion," Kayla said, "and not his fascination with you."

Inaya's eyebrows shot up at her cousin's bluntness. "His fascination with *me*?"

"Oh come on, Inaya." Kayla rolled her eyes and shook her head. "It's clear you two really hit it off."

Inaya turned her head toward the side window to suppress a grin. Really? Was it possible that she wasn't living on false hopes?

"But I trust Raymond." Kayla's tone sounded conflicted. Kayla propped an elbow on the window next to her as she slowed the car at a four-way-stop. "I don't think he would cheat on Lyrica," she said before guiding the car forward again. "They've been together for three years, and he's always been faithful."

Inaya felt offended at her cousin's words. But she couldn't think of that right then. She just wondered what she would say if Raymond called...

If her mother or stepfather didn't answer first.

# 10

# The Call

"Inaya, the phone is for you."

Veronica stood in the doorway to Inaya's room Friday night holding the cordless phone.

Heart racing, Inaya nervously turned to her mother. But Inaya could not read her mother's expression. Veronica's hair was disheveled, apparently from sleeping on it, and Veronica looked exhausted. Inaya had heard Abdullah crying all afternoon and evening, and she remembered her mother saying that Abdullah was running a slight fever.

If Veronica had heard a male voice on the other end of the line, she probably was too sleep-deprived to notice or register what it meant.

Inaya raised herself from the chair and took the phone from her mother. Her heart raced as she counted the three seconds it took her mother to leave and close the door. Inaya leaned against the wall momentarily and cradled the phone to her chest as she drew in a deep breath and exhaled.

She glanced at the clock. It was 9:37. It was late but not too late. She slid back into her desk chair and put the phone to her ear.

"Hello?" She spoke as calmly as she could, but she detected a quiver in her voice.

"Inaya?"

At the sound of a girl's voice, Inaya's heart sank. She grew irritated. Who was calling her at this time of night?

"Yes..." Inaya said tentatively.

"Oh my God, I finally got through."

Inaya drew her brows together at the sound of a British accent. "Who's this?"

"This is Rafa," the girl said.

The image of Inaya's best friend from Saudi Arabia was so disconnected from Inaya's life in America that Inaya had forgotten about her. Inaya's heart fell in disappointment. She wasn't in the mood to talk to Rafa, but Inaya felt guilty for feeling this way.

"*As-salaamu 'alaikum*," Rafa said, laughter in her voice, her excitement palpable through the receiver. "My parents finally agreed to let me have an internet phone."

"*Wa'alaiku-mus-salaam.*" Inaya hoped she sounded more excited than she felt. But in that brief moment, Inaya felt a tinge of sadness for what she had left behind when she moved to America. "That's so good, *maashaAllah*."

"Yeah, I know." Rafa giggled. "Now I can call you all the time."

Inaya leaned her elbows on the desk and toyed with a pen. "That's really good."

"I know!"

Rafa sighed. "Oh, you have to tell me everything. How is it? Are you homesick yet?"

Inaya laughed beside herself, and Rafa laughed too. But Inaya knew Rafa couldn't imagine why Inaya found the question amusing.

"It's good. I'm…" Inaya's voice trailed as she realized there was nothing she felt comfortable confiding to Rafa. "…in school now."

"That's so cool. Is it that Saudi school in Virginia?"

Inaya contorted her face, but she maintained her polite tone. "No, it's…closer."

"My cousin's wife told me they have a lot of Muslim schools there," Rafa said.

Rafa sighed again. "I wish we could visit the States."

Inaya drew her head back in surprise. "Why?"

"I hear it's really beautiful there, and the people are nice."

Inaya nodded as she thought about her experience so far. "Well, that's true."

"So tell me everything," Rafa said anxiously. "How is Muslim school in America?"

Before Inaya could respond, Rafa continued. "I'm trying to convince my mother to let me stay with my uncle after I finish my O levels, but she thinks I'll get corrupted or something." Rafa groaned. "She thinks I'll take off my hijab and become Americanized."

Inaya's cheeks grew warm, and she fought the inclination to say something in her own defense. But that wouldn't make any sense because Rafa had no idea she had offended Inaya.

"I go to public school," Inaya said finally, "but they have a club for Muslim students."

Rafa sucked in her breath in surprise. "Are you serious? Oh my God. I bet you get to do all sorts of *da'wah*."

Inaya thought of Raymond's and Lyrica's interest in religion and the conversation she'd had with her father. "Yeah, I get to teach people about Islam."

"Are you still studying Qur'an?"

"I'm a teacher at a Muslim weekend school."

"You're a *Qur'an* teacher?" Inaya could sense Rafa's awe and amazement through the phone, and for a moment Inaya saw herself through Rafa's eyes.

It was chilling how the truth could be so deceptive. Was this the same half-truth Inaya had created for herself when she'd said she couldn't wait to move back to America? But at the time, it hadn't occurred to Inaya herself that she would struggle as a Muslim in the States.

"Yes," Inaya said finally, her tone devoid of emotion despite her effort to sound enthusiastic.

*"Living in a Muslim country makes you a weak Muslim."* These were the words that came to Inaya right then. It was something her Saudi friend Batool had said once.

*"That's not true,"* Inaya had shot back, offended.

*"In America, the Muslims are stronger,"* Batool insisted. *"They cover and pray and fast, and they don't care what people think."* When Inaya contended that Batool was mistaken, Batool had rolled her eyes and said, *"Show me someone from a Muslim country who's like that. They don't want to even be seen in hijab."*

"See," Rafa said with a sigh, reminding Inaya that her friend was still on the phone. "That's what I keep telling my mom. I can get an American diploma in the States and still practice Islam. But sh—paranoid."

A beeping sound disrupted Rafa's sentence.

"Hold on a second," Inaya told Rafa. "There's a call on the other line."

Inaya pulled the phone from her face and pressed the flash button.

"Hello?" she said after putting the phone back to her ear.

"Yes, good evening," a deep voice greeted. "May I speak to Inaya please?"

Inaya's heart raced as she recognized the sound of Raymond's voice.

"One moment please," she said. Her hands trembled as she clicked back over to Rafa.

"Rafa?"

"Yeah, I'm still here."

"I have to go." Inaya sighed her apology, feigning regret at having to cut the conversation so short. "It's an important call…for my family."

"No problem," Rafa said. "Can I call after an hour?" She laughed. "I have *so* much to tell you."

"Um…" Inaya's heart grew heavy in dread. "…sure."

A thought came to Inaya just then. "Maybe I should just call you back when I'm free."

"Oh, that would be great," Rafa said. "It's early morning here and I'll be home."

"Is this your number on the caller I.D.?"

"Yes," Rafa said. "It's our American internet phone."

"Okay, cool," Inaya said. "*Insha'Allah*, I'll call you when I'm done." She shut her eyes and shook her head. "When I'm free, I mean."

"I'll wait for your call."

Rafa sounded so enthusiastic that Inaya felt sick with guilt. She had no intention to call Rafa back, but she imagined that she had no other choice.

"No one else uses this phone," Rafa said, giddy excitement in her voice. "It's mine to talk to my cousins and friends in America."

"That's nice," Inaya said, growing frustrated. She hated keeping Raymond waiting. What if he hung up?

"Oh yeah," Rafa said, as if recalling something just then. "Did you hear Batool is engaged?"

Inaya gritted her teeth and glanced at the clock. "Rafa, I have to go." Inaya felt bad for being rude, but she had already told Rafa that there was an important call waiting. She was losing patience. If Raymond got disconnected, she would never forgive her friend.

"Oh...okay." The defeated sound in Rafa's voice made Inaya ashamed of herself. But she wasn't about to apologize.

"I'll wait for your call," Rafa said quietly.

"*As-salaamu 'alaikum*," Inaya said, pressing the flash button before Rafa had a chance to reply.

"Raymond?" Inaya said, struggling to catch her breath.

There was silence on the other end of the receiver, and for a second Inaya's heart stopped. Had he hung up?

"Yes..." a cautious voice said finally.

It was then that Inaya realized that he had never said who he was—and she hadn't either. For all he knew, it was Inaya's mother who'd answered the phone. Her face grew hot in embarrassment.

"This is Inaya," she said quickly. "I had to hang up another call."

"Oh, I'm sorry," he said. "I can call back later. I didn't mean to disturb you."

"No, it's okay. I was finished anyway."

"Okay good."

There was an awkward pause as Inaya had no idea what to say next. She had no experience with things like this.

"I hope it's not too late," Raymond said.

"No, no." Inaya mentally scolded herself for sounding eager to talk. "I'm wide awake."

"I guess Kayla told you she gave me your number."

"Yeah… She mentioned something like that."

"I hope you don't mind…"

"Not at all." Inaya drew in a deep breath to steady her short breaths. "I'm fine with it. Anytime."

"Good."

There was a brief pause.

"I wanted to talk to you …" he said hesitantly, and Inaya's heart raced as he spoke. "…because the school asked Student Council to form a committee of students to act as liaisons and public relations representatives for the school."

Inaya slumped back into her chair, defeated, disinterested all of a sudden.

"They asked me to chair it," Raymond said with a sigh. "But to be honest, with all my duties at school and my scholarship applications to fill out and college essays to write when I'm home, I don't think I can take on anything else."

"Mm, hm," Inaya said, half-listening.

"So I thought of you."

Inaya creased her forehead. "For what?"

"To chair the committee."

It was then that Inaya began to process what he was asking.

"But…what about Lyrica?" The question came out more resentful than Inaya had intended.

"She's taking courses at a community college after school," he said, his tone cautious, "so she wants to focus on that."

*Oh*, Inaya thought numbly. So he *did* ask his girlfriend first. Inaya was only an afterthought.

Inaya felt drained all of a sudden. She needed to pray *'Ishaa*. It was the oddest moment to desire spiritual connection, but she was so confused lately. She needed a moment to gather her thoughts.

Inaya wished she hadn't rushed Rafa off the phone. Maybe Rafa could give her some advice…even if Inaya could never reveal to Rafa why she needed it.

"I don't know, Raymond." Inaya sighed. "I have a lot going on."

"I know…" His voice sounded disappointed, and Inaya felt bad.

"I just don't think I'm the right person for the job."

Raymond chuckled. "Well, that's where you're wrong."

Inaya's spirits lifted slightly, enjoying the positive attention, even if only momentary. "I don't think so," she said with a smirk.

"Inaya," he said, and Inaya's face grew warm at the sound of his voice saying her name, "I gave this a lot of thought. And there's really no one else I can think of who's better than you."

"Not even Lyrica?" Inaya teased. At the sound of his laughter through the receiver, Inaya smiled.

"Think about it, okay?" he said finally.

It didn't escape Inaya that he didn't answer her last question.

"But I'll give your name to the Student Affairs Office on Monday."

Before Inaya could protest, he continued.

"Don't worry," he said. "It's not a commitment. Just a suggestion."

"Okay," Inaya said, sighing. "If you say so."

"You can turn it down if you like," he said.

She chuckled. "Thanks."

"No," he said. "Thank *you*. You're truly a lifesaver."

# 11

# On Board

"Who's the boss?"

Inaya felt someone nudge her as she walked in step with Mrs. Ford, who, like Inaya, was carrying an armful of binders as they hurried down the hall to the Student Affairs Office.

Inaya and Mrs. Ford turned and found Raymond smiling at them.

The Monday following Raymond's phone call, Inaya had told Raymond during lunch that she would give the student committee position a try. Now it was Tuesday, just over two weeks since her agreement, and she was already overwhelmed. She had decided to stay after school today to meet with Mrs. Ford, the faculty advisor to the student committee board.

"You're the boss," Raymond answered himself, playfully pointing at Inaya.

Inaya grinned beside herself. "Thanks to you." She rolled her eyes playfully.

Raymond nodded then patted Inaya on the shoulder. "We'll do great things together," he said before pushing open an exit door and offering a wave.

"What was that about?" Mrs. Ford asked after the heavy exit door closed behind Raymond and she and Inaya neared the Student Affairs Office.

"It's a private joke about us," Inaya said, smiling to herself.

Mrs. Ford raised her eyebrows suspiciously as she kneeled in front of her office door to set the stack of binders on the floor. "About you and Raymond?"

Inaya creased her forehead then laughed as she realized how her response sounded to the faculty advisor. She shook her head.

"I mean you and me," Inaya said. "Well, the whole student board actually."

Keys jingled as Mrs. Ford found the one for her office and unlocked the door.

"Really?" A confused grin was on Mrs. Ford's face as she pushed open the door and met Inaya's gaze.

"B-O-S-S," Inaya said as she walked into the office ahead of Mrs. Ford and let the binders spill onto the front desk. She looked back over her shoulder to smile at Mrs. Ford, who was now entering carrying the stack of binders she'd set outside the door.

"It's the unofficial acronym for the name I gave the board," Inaya said.

Mrs. Ford's expression was of thoughtful humor as she tried to grasp what Inaya was saying.

"Board of Student Statesmen," Inaya said. "Raymond said it sounds like some sexist, male-dominated political group."

Mrs. Ford laughed as she walked around her desk and settled into her office chair. She propped an elbow on her desk and rested a loose fist beneath her chin, intrigued as Inaya explained.

"He says women are the real bosses in the group." Inaya sat down on a folding chair against a wall, laughter in her voice. "So every time he sees me, he says, 'Who's the BOSS?'"

Inaya sighed, a smile lingering on her face. "But it's also his way of saying females make guys think that men are running things." She folded her arms in front of her. "While women secretly plot to run even the guys."

Mrs. Ford's eyes widened in amusement. "He told you that?"

"Yes," Inaya said, her eyes sparkling with laughter, "but not in those words."

Mrs. Ford grinned as she reached for a binder and opened it, her eyes scanning its content. "Well, I must admit, he does have a point."

Inaya shrugged. "I guess so."

An awkward silence followed as Mrs. Ford flipped through the pages of the binder.

"But I think his little private joke is more private than you think."

Inaya creased her forehead, an uncomfortable smile on her face. "What do you mean?"

Mrs. Ford wore a pleasant expression as she skimmed the last part of the binder then closed it. When she did not respond immediately, Inaya thought Mrs. Ford had not heard the question.

"Inaya," Mrs. Ford said as she met Inaya's gaze, "you do know why I didn't agree to have Lyrica chair the board, don't you?"

Inaya's smile faded until her eyebrows were knitted in confusion. Inaya parted her lips to form the question that was in her mind, but she realized there were no words for it.

"I'm not sure how much Raymond told you," Mrs. Ford said, as if deciding it was better to be frank than polite. She met Inaya's perplexed expression with a gentle smile. "But it was Lyrica's idea to start this committee."

Inaya's mouth fell open in shock. "But I thought…"

Mrs. Ford waved her hand dismissively. "I know what you thought. And it's partly true." She nodded. "The school did ask Raymond to help form this committee."

When Inaya did not speak, Mrs. Ford continued.

"But that was only because we knew Lyrica was not the right person for the job." Mrs. Ford drew in a deep breath and exhaled.

"Yes, we liked Lyrica's idea," she said. "But we had some ideas of our own. And, well…" She smiled apologetically. "Let's just say, we didn't think they matched Lyrica's."

Inaya found herself wondering at the faculty advisor's use of the pronoun *we*. Inaya shook her head. "I'm sorry. I don't understand…"

Mrs. Ford glanced thoughtfully toward the curtain that divided her office and the humble photo studio Inaya had entered to take her school picture. Inaya could tell the faculty advisor was deciding the best way to explain what she meant.

"Lyrica's an atheist," Mrs. Ford said finally. She met Inaya's gaze sadly. "And frankly, we find that offensive."

Inaya nodded slowly, but she had a sinking feeling that she herself had to be careful of offending Mrs. Ford.

"Yes, this is a public school," Mrs. Ford said. "But our obligation to separate church from state doesn't make us sacrilegious. We were originally a private Christian school, and it was only in the last twenty years that it was shut down then reopened as a state-funded institution."

Mrs. Ford sighed, her gaze distant momentarily. "We couldn't afford to keep it private, and we regret that," she said. "But our mission remains to keep God as a foundational part of the learning experience here."

Mrs. Ford smiled at Inaya, as if that kind expression would explain everything—as if she and Inaya were on the same page.

"And that means seeing to it that those who represent us are only God-fearing Christians."

"But…" Inaya's mind raced. "What about the Distinguished Student Award?"

Part of the role of the student board was to make recommendations to teachers and administration regarding outstanding students who might have otherwise been overlooked. Naturally, student recommendations did not affect the school's final decision in any official capacity, but Mrs. Ford assured Inaya and the board members that their suggestions would be taken seriously. Was Inaya now to approve only Christian students?

"We have to exclude other religions?" Inaya hoped she didn't sound as exasperated as she felt.

Mrs. Ford smiled, but Inaya sensed the faculty advisor was enjoying a private joke herself. "Of course not," Mrs. Ford said, but Inaya heard the obligatory tone of Mrs. Ford's voice. "But that would be ideal."

Inaya forced a smile, but she didn't know what to say.

"But you have nothing to worry about," Mrs. Ford said. "As far as I'm concerned, you're our first choice."

Inaya met Mrs. Ford's gaze with her eyes widened. She opened her mouth to protest, but no sound came out.

"But no need to worry about all that now." A grin formed on Mrs. Ford's face as she handed a binder to Inaya. "For now, we're just happy to have you on board."

# 12

## The Reward

Saturday morning Inaya stood in front of the classroom full of Muslim children, the Qur'an open in her hands. She raised her voice as she recited from the first chapter entitled *Al-Faatihah*, the Opening, and in unison the children repeated after her.

It had taken three classes and many restless nights, but Inaya finally found a way to keep the children's attention. She would walk between the rows of desks telling them stories and asking them prompting questions. The stories were always related to the part of Qur'an they were studying at the time, and Inaya often supplemented the story with colorful posters and exaggerated hand gestures and sound effects. Sometimes she allowed the students out of their seats to participate.

"Imagine," she said after they finished reciting and she returned the Qur'an to her desk. "Imagine your parents said you could have all the toys and treasures you want and you could do whatever you wanted forever and ever."

The students grinned. Some whispered in excitement to their friends about what they would do if that happened.

"Raise your hand if you would like that, if you'd like your parents to tell you that."

Hands shot up, and some girls and boys bounced up and down in their seats as they waved their hands in the air. "Me, Sister Inaya! I would like that!"

"Imagine they said you could eat whatever candy and cookies and ice cream and cake you wanted!"

"Ooooh!"

"Would you like that?" Inaya smiled as their eyes sparkled in excitement.

"Awesome!"

"And they said you could have *all* of this," Inaya said, her eyes widening, "if you do just *one* thing." She raised her forefinger for emphasis. "Would you do what they asked you?"

"Yes!" the class shouted emphatically.

"But what if…" Inaya frowned as she paced the room in front of them. "What if somebody said no? What if they said, 'No, I won't do what you asked me'?"

"Well, that's stupid," one boy said, grunting as he folded his arms in front of him.

"But why would they say no?" a girl asked, her face tortured in confusion.

"Well, because they were too tired to do it," Inaya said. "Or maybe they just didn't want to."

"But it's just *one* thing," the girl said, a plea in her voice.

"Nobody would say no!" the boy shouted in angry frustration, as if challenging the teacher herself.

Inaya smiled and shook her head. "Lots of people would say no. Lots and lots."

"Nuh uh." Several children shook their heads. "Not me."

"Well," Inaya said, tilting her head thoughtfully, "Allah promises us more than toys, cookies, candy, and ice cream." She smiled at them, and they listened attentively. "He promises us Paradise—*Jannah*."

She drew in a deep breath and exhaled. "But lots of people say no," she said. "And to get this reward, all He asked us to do is believe in Him until we die."

\*\*\*

As the children scurried out the classroom, Inaya collapsed into the teacher's chair in front of the room, her heart heavy.

"Bye, Sister Inaya!" a girl shouted from the door.

Inaya forced a smile and lifted her hand in a wave. "*As-salaamu'alaikum*, Reem."

*And that means seeing to it that those who represent us are only God-fearing Christians.*

These words stayed with Inaya for four full days, and they kept her awake at night. But it wasn't until she was reciting *Al-Faatihah* with the children that Inaya understood her anxiety.

Inaya had never said to Mrs. Ford that she was Christian. But from the day that Inaya entered Mrs. Ford's office to take her I.D. picture, she'd purposefully avoided mentioning that she was Muslim.

When Inaya found herself working with Mrs. Ford for up to three hours after school, it was only natural that they talked about their lives every now and then. Though Mrs. Ford did not open up much when she first met Inaya, over time the faculty advisor began to talk openly about God and the importance of faith in one's life. It was a topic that appealed to Inaya deeply, and Inaya found herself sharing her own thoughts and experiences—without mentioning Islam.

It was amazing to Inaya how much she and Mrs. Ford had in common, and Inaya began to look forward to sitting with the faculty advisor after school. It was the only time Inaya actually felt like herself, the only time she almost forgot that she was different. Almost everything they talked about centered on the concept of sincere submission to God—the English translation of the word *Islam*.

There were moments that Inaya had been tempted to mention Islam openly and ask Mrs. Ford if she had studied the religion because there was so much that Mrs. Ford was saying that mirrored Muslim beliefs.

"Are you saved?" Mrs. Ford had asked Inaya once.

Inaya had laughed uncomfortably. "I hope so. But I think only God can answer that for me."

Mrs. Ford nodded. "That's what my husband and I always say. Being saved is not something you choose. It's something God chooses."

Inaya had not intended to imply that she was Christian. She had only wished to avoid saying that she was Muslim. So whenever Mrs. Ford mentioned Jesus as the son of God, Inaya would remain silent.

But as Inaya sat in front of her Qur'an class, she realized that there was one conversation where she had gone too far.

One day, in the midst of preparing notes for an upcoming meeting, Mrs. Ford had asked what church Inaya attended—and Inaya mentioned the name of the church her family had attended when she was a child.

"But we don't go there much anymore," Inaya had added quickly. "After my parents got divorced, church sort of left our lives."

"Well," Mrs. Ford said, "what's most important is that it didn't leave your heart."

Inaya had felt uncomfortable with the comment, and it had taken her a full minute to think of a proper response. "To be honest," Inaya told Mrs. Ford, "after the divorce, the only thing that didn't leave my heart is God." She smiled at Mrs. Ford. "And He's not confined to a church."

That was the closest Inaya had come to saying that she wasn't Christian. But Inaya knew that it wasn't close enough.

***

Inaya glanced at her watch as she sat in the last row of chairs reserved for teachers in the gymnasium at the Muslim weekend school. She hoped her mother wouldn't be late picking her up. Inaya had wanted to leave immediately after class, but there was an award ceremony for the students. Inaya knew it would appear rude if she was not present to give her students their awards. But her class had received their awards twenty minutes ago, and her mother had still not arrived.

"…Inaya Donald."

There was a roar of applause, and Inaya brought her hands together as she looked around in search of who'd called her name.

"She was always a very modest teacher," a voice said through the speakers. "So I'm sure she imagines this award is for another Inaya Donald."

Stunned, Inaya looked toward the front of the gymnasium and saw that Sister Amal was standing in front of the microphone holding a framed certificate.

"Yes, Inaya," Sister Amal said, "this award is for you, our most outstanding teacher."

*But…*

Inaya felt her legs go weak. What was Sister Amal talking about? Inaya hadn't paid any attention to the program. The voices had become background noise as she counted down the minutes until she could go home.

"We love you, Sister Inaya!" some of her students shouted.

Somehow Inaya found the strength to stand, but on shaky legs. She cautiously walked to the front of the gymnasium— to accept an award she knew she didn't deserve.

And it did not escape her that some of her fellow teachers, who were all elder to her, felt the same. Though they clapped, their expressions were of resentment, and Inaya did not want to believe the sinking feeling that it wasn't due only to her young age.

"Inaya is our youngest teacher here," Sister Amal said into the microphone, beaming. "And she's also our only American."

Inaya wore a frozen smile as she neared the microphone, her heart drumming in her chest. She felt the beginning of a headache as she saw the scrutinizing stares of the audience.

"She's a junior in high school and attends public school. Her parents converted to Islam when she was a child, and she memorized Qur'an at the age of thirteen."

There were hoots and cries of *Allahu'akbar!* But Inaya felt the envious stares of her colleagues.

"And her mother was kind enough to let me speak to some of Inaya's friends from Saudi Arabia," Sister Amal said, sending Inaya's heart racing as Inaya halted her steps next to Sister Amal.

"And *maashaAllah*," Sister Amal said, "I think the poem they wrote for her tells us that she was a blessing to them too."

Inaya's eyes widened, and she had to resist the urge to snatch the paper from Sister Amal's hand.

"And this was written in the heart of the Muslim world by girls who were Arab, Pakistani, Indian, British and American," Sister Amal said, a proud grin on her face, "and that alone should tell us the immense blessing we have in having Inaya amongst us."

Sister Amal turned to smile at Inaya, and Inaya dropped her head, unable to meet Sister Amal's gaze.

"And I think I speak for all of us when I say these words are a message and an inspiration to all Muslims."

The hushed silence in the gymnasium was a clear sign that hearing this poem would not be a surprise only to Inaya, but to the entire community of Muslims present that day.

*We have no idea what we're going to do without you,*
*"The girl who gets things done."*
*But I suppose we'll have to figure out a way to still learn,*
*Do things right, and have some fun!*
*Thanks for teaching us the meaning of friendship*

*And love for Allah's sake.*
*Thanks for telling us to pray and cover—*
*Without taking a break!*
*Thanks for teaching us that Islam is a religion of action,*
*Not a religion of words.*
*Thanks for reminding us that saying*
*No! to Allah (about anything) is absurd.*
*We're going to miss you, Inaya,*
*Our beloved sister, "cousin", and friend.*
*But like you always say, "Keep the faith, girl,*
*And, insha'Allah, we'll meet in the End."*

***

"Congratulations."

Inaya was trailing behind her mother in the parking lot of the Muslim school when she heard this word for the umpteenth time. She already knew that whoever was speaking was talking to her, but Inaya had no desire to turn around and acknowledge their presence. Inaya was exhausted, mentally and physically, and she doubted she could last another minute at the school.

Veronica turned and smiled, halting her steps to shake the person's hand.

"Are you Sister Amal's daughter?" Inaya heard her mother say. "You look just like her."

"Yes," the soft voice replied. "I go to school with Inaya."

At these words, Inaya jerked her head in the direction of the speaker and halted her own steps—and she found herself looking into the eyes of Nasra.

Nasra smiled at Inaya, a smile that told Inaya that Nasra knew her secret—and that Inaya would never be safe.

"*As-salaamu'alaikum*, Inaya," Nasra said cheerfully as she reached out to shake Inaya's limp hand.

"I can't say I'm surprised, *maashaAllah*," Nasra said, her words sending Inaya's heart racing. "Like I told you," she said with a smile, "I always knew you were someone special."

## 13

## An Example

"But couldn't you have asked me first?" Inaya stood in front of the stove stirring the spaghetti sauce she was preparing for dinner that Saturday evening. Her mother sat at the kitchen table shredding cheese as she nursed Abdullah, who was hidden beneath the small blanket that lay over Veronica's shoulder.

"I wanted it to be a surprise," Veronica said.

Inaya glanced over her shoulder and saw the look of satisfaction on her mother's face. Inaya gritted her teeth and turned back to the stove.

"It was…embarrassing," Inaya said.

Veronica laughed. "You're too humble, sweetheart." She shook her head. "But now you're an example to all those stuck-up Arabs and Pakistanis."

Inaya flinched at the cruel words, but she could think of no intelligent response.

"They always think they know Islam better than us." Veronica huffed. "But most of their children don't even pray or cover."

Inaya stiffened in anger. Was that what this was about? Proving to the "cultural Muslims" that the Americans were better? That the converts were the only "real Muslims"?

"They walk around looking and acting like *kaafir*s." Veronica twisted her face in contempt. "They even have boyfriends and girlfriends."

It took a moment for Inaya to gather her composure enough to speak. "All Muslims struggle, Mom," Inaya said, her voice shaky from nervousness and annoyance. "Nobody's perfect."

"Yes, nobody's perfect," Veronica said, a smug grin on her face as she glanced at Inaya. "But at least we're not ashamed to tell the world we're Muslim." She grunted. "But these people do everything they can to hide it."

Inaya's face grew warm, and she became overwhelmed with shame.

Quietly, Inaya stirred the sauce until large bubbles surfaced. Steam rose and warmed her chin, and she wished her family had never left Saudi Arabia. Inaya never imagined that she would become so weak, and so quickly. She thought of Nasra and wondered at the girl's strength and faith. How did she do it? And with so much ease…

The shrilling of a phone interrupted Inaya's thoughts.

"Can you get that, Inaya?" Veronica said, turning to her daughter. "It's probably Anisa saying she's on her way."

\*\*\*

"Inaya, *maashaAllah*!" Veronica's best friend beamed as she stood at the front door of the apartment studying Inaya as she held Inaya's hands.

Anisa still wore her voluminous black *jilbaab* that hung from the top of her head and fell to her ankles. Her face veil was flipped back, revealing the honey brown of her face, which seemed to glow next to her dark brown eyes lined in black eyeliner and mascara.

"You've grown so much," Anisa said as she squeezed Inaya's hands before letting go.

Inaya smiled, unsure what to say as she stepped aside to let Sister Anisa inside.

"*As-salaamu 'alaikum*, stranger," Veronica said after emerging from the kitchen. She wiped her hands on her shirt before drawing her friend into a hug. "I thought you were avoiding me or something."

Anisa laughed and shook her head. "You were always the paranoid type." She sighed. "Driving forty minutes in my car is definitely not my idea of a good time."

"I guess I should've come to you then," Veronica said after releasing Anisa.

"Oh please," Anisa said, waving her hand. "And drag that poor baby out the house for nothing? I wouldn't let you even if you offered."

Anisa glanced around. "Where is he anyway?"

"He's sleeping," Veronica said with a smile. "But don't worry, he'll wake up in a few minutes *insha'Allah*. Then you'll wish he was asleep."

The friends laughed as Inaya closed the door and locked it, a polite smile on her face.

"Are you hungry?" Veronica asked as Anisa removed her *jilbaab*, revealing a long-sleeved T-shirt and wide-legged jeans, her face still framed by a black *khimaar*.

Anisa shook her head as she handed her *jilbaab* and face veil to Inaya. "Not yet. Right now, the only thing I'm craving is your company."

Inaya hung Anisa's *jilbaab* on the coatrack then started for the hallway that led to her room.

"Oh, Inaya," Anisa said, prompting Inaya to turn around. "Sit with me before you disappear to do whatever it is you teenagers do nowadays."

Inaya hesitated as she thought of all the homework she had to do, and the work for the BOSS club.

"Okay," she said finally. She followed Anisa to the couch.

"Did you hear about the award Inaya won today?"

Inaya's face grew warm at the pride in her mother's voice. Veronica settled into the recliner across from them, and Inaya avoided her mother's gaze as she sat down a comfortable distance from Anisa. But Inaya maintained a stiff smile similar to the one she wore when she'd accepted the award.

Anisa lifted her eyebrows in pleasant interest then shook her head. "No, I didn't."

"The Muslim weekend school has this mid-semester award ceremony every year," Veronica said, unable to keep from grinning widely. "And they choose the most outstanding teacher and—"

"No!" Anisa interjected, laughter in her voice as she looked at Inaya. "Are you serious?"

Veronica nodded. "Dead serious."

"*MaashaAllah*," Anisa said, shaking her head in admiration of Inaya.

"I was so happy to see how shocked all those Arabs and Pakistanis were."

Anisa drew her eyebrows together as she met her friend's gaze, smile fading. "What do you mean?"

"Inaya's the only Black person there," Veronica said, pride in her voice. "The only American actually." She grunted. "Unless you count the handful of White women who come to pick up their children after class." She waved her hand dismissively. "But most of them aren't even Muslim."

Anisa frowned momentarily then looked at Inaya. "That's a lot of pressure for a sixteen-year-old," she said.

Inaya was surprised to see sympathy in Anisa's eyes.

"Are you sure it's a good idea for her to teach there?" Anisa added.

Veronica contorted her face and glared at Anisa. "Of course it's a good idea. They need to see what a real Muslim looks like."

An awkward silence followed as Veronica folded her arms. "I'm tired of all their stupid racism."

"But..." Anisa looked troubled as she glanced uncertainly at Inaya. "...isn't Inaya in school now? I mean—"

"Oh come on, Anisa." Veronica rolled her eyes. "Leave it to you to make me feel bad about the first good thing that's happened to us in months."

Inaya lowered her gaze at her mother's use of the pronoun *us*. Though Inaya was flattered to have received the award, she didn't think of it as a good thing, at least not right then. She wished her mother hadn't talked to Rafa behind her back. If only her mother knew how humiliated she felt…

"I'm sorry, Ronnie," Anisa said, her voice apologetic. "It's just that I remember how much pressure my parents put on me when I was growing up, and—"

"Your parents weren't following the *Sunnah*," Veronica said with a grunt, referring to the prophetic example. "So of course you grew up under pressure."

Anisa widened her eyes in shock. "What?" She shook her head, a wounded expression on her face. "That has nothing to do with what I'm saying."

"Inaya isn't like you were," Veronica said. "She knows her *deen*."

"Come on, Ronnie," Anisa said, her voice a plea of reason. "Even if my parents knew the *Sunnah* after they became Muslim, it wouldn't have made my life easier."

"The *Sunnah* is balanced, Anisa," Veronica said. "Your parents asked you to be fully American while you practiced Islam." She shook her head. "The only difference between you and the next *kaafir* was an African wrap on your head."

Anisa's jaw dropped, and Inaya felt as if she were intruding on a private conversation. She wondered if she should leave to her room.

"And that *head-wrap*," Anisa said sarcastically, "was the barrier between me and a normal life."

Anisa contorted her face as she regarded her friend. "You really surprise me, Ronnie. Do you really think Islam is about wearing all black, covering your face, and putting your hands in the right position when you pray?"

"I don't trivialize *any* part of Islam," Veronica retorted. "To me, all those things are what Islam is about."

"Then you're wrong, *ukhti*," Anisa said. "Dead wrong."

Anisa shook her head. "Islam is about only one thing, and that's believing in Allah and holding on to that until you die."

Veronica raised her eyebrows skeptically. "And you actually believe we don't have to do anything about that belief?"

"Of course we do," Anisa said. "But nobody's perfect. Nobody can do everything right."

"But we should try."

"Yes, we *should*," Anisa said. "But we're human, so most of us won't put in the effort we should."

Veronica wrinkled her nose as she glanced at Inaya. "I refuse to teach my daughter that defeatist ideology."

"It's not defeatist, *ukhti*." Anisa lowered her voice, as if trying to reason with her friend. "It's reality."

"Then what's the point of being Muslim if I don't put any work into it?"

Anisa narrowed her eyes as she regarded Veronica. "You really don't get it, do you?"

Unsure what to say, Veronica met her friend's gaze unblinking, a defiant expression on her face.

"The greatest work you can put into being Muslim isn't in your clothes or the school of thought you follow," Anisa said. "It's in your heart." She shook her head. "And no *jilbaab* or *niqaab* or scholar can help you if you don't work on your heart."

A thoughtful silence settled over the room.

"I know that," Veronica said finally. "But you can't fix your heart without obeying Allah."

Anisa nodded. "But we all sin."

Veronica rolled her eyes. "That's the same old song these foreign Muslims sing when they do wrong."

"But I'm not talking about them, Ronnie," Anisa said as she glanced at Inaya. "I'm talking about us, all of us."

Anisa sighed. "Till today," she said, "I wonder how differently my life would have turned out if my parents hadn't made me think I had to be an example to the world."

At these words, Inaya turned to her mother's friend, interest piqued. But Anisa's gaze was distant as she looked at something beyond the living room.

"I wish they had just told me the truth."

Inaya stole a glance at her mother, but Veronica's expression was hard to read. Veronica was nibbling at her lower lip, her eyes on her hands folded loosely in her lap.

"That the best I could hope for was just dying as a believer," Anisa said.

She shook her head. "I wish I knew I didn't have to be an example to *anyone*," Anisa said, her voice barely above a whisper as she emphasized the last word. "Except myself."

# 14

# Hope

"Good luck," Mr. Rhodes said as Inaya followed the other students out the homeroom class one Monday morning in mid-December.

Inaya creased her forehead as she halted her steps to meet his gaze. "I'm sorry?"

"Good luck," he repeated as he smiled and handed Inaya a white envelope.

"What's this?" she said as she accepted the envelope cautiously. She glanced at her full name printed neatly on the front. *Inaya Christina Donald.*

"You're one of the finalists for the Distinguished Student Award."

Inaya grew beside herself in excitement. What if she actually won? But she maintained her composure as she smiled at Mr. Rhodes. "Thanks."

"This nomination makes you automatically eligible for the Future Hope Scholarship," he said. "You'll find instructions inside for applying."

"Thanks." Inaya was unable to keep from grinning.

As soon as she was in the hallway, she tore open the envelope and eagerly read its contents.

To the Parents of Inaya Christina Donald:

It is with great pleasure that we inform you that your daughter has been nominated for our school's Distinguished Student Award. Each year, we select one student for this honor based on his/her outstanding academic achievement and specific recommendation by administration, faculty, and fellow students.

The student who is chosen receives a $1000 award to be remitted after he/she is eighteen years old. However, all nominees are eligible for the Future Hope Scholarship, which funds up to four years of the student's undergraduate studies for up to $25,000 a year.

If your son/daughter is chosen as our Distinguished Student this year, he/she will receive the Distinguished Student's Scholarship, which funds up to eight years of the student's education and college fees for up to $30,000 a year for undergraduate studies and up to $50,000 a year for graduate studies...

Inaya screamed in excitement and immediately cupped her hand over her mouth in embarrassment as she noticed students glancing at her curiously.

Still smiling, Inaya quickly folded the papers and returned them to the envelope before stuffing the envelope into her backpack. She couldn't wait to get home to tell her mother.

\*\*\*

"I hope they don't skip over you because you're Muslim," Veronica said as she leaned against the wall next to the foyer. She had just finished reading all the contents of the envelope that Inaya had handed to her.

Inaya was still wearing her black *jilbaab* and pink *khimaar* she had put on before getting in the car with Kayla. Her cheeks grew warm as she looked at her mother.

"I don't think they'd do that." But Inaya's voice was subdued as she thought of her conversations with Mrs. Ford.

"Well," Veronica said as Inaya slipped off the outer-garment and hijab and hung them on the coat stand by the door, "it says this is sponsored by Future Hope Baptist Church."

"Really?" Inaya reached for the papers and took them from her mother, heart racing. The name of the church sounded familiar...

Inaya's eyes skimmed the part of the letter that she hadn't bothered to read, and sure enough, there it was, the name of the church that Mrs. Ford attended. Inaya's heart sank as she realized her chances were slim.

"If you do win," Veronica said, "I think it would be really good for *da'wah*."

Inaya creased her forehead. "How?"

Veronica pointed to the papers in Inaya's hand. "It says the award ceremony is covered by local news stations and is posted on the school's YouTube channel," Veronica said. "Imagine the whole world seeing a Muslim girl accept that award."

Veronica smiled and patted Inaya softly on the cheek. "You would make the world proud, Inaya." She shook her head. "May Allah bless it for you."

*\*\*\**

Alone in her room, Inaya sat at her desk, the three pages of the nomination letter spread out in front of her. Her hand trembled as her eyes scanned the words on the bottom of the first page: "...sponsored annually by Future Hope Baptist Church in Potomac, Maryland."

But it was the second page that concerned her most.

Each year, the award ceremony is covered by three local television news channels, five local newspapers, and one national online publication. It is also streamed lived on our school's website and subsequently posted on our YouTube channel. Additionally, Future Hope Baptist Church hosts a scholarship dinner and radio show to interview the winner...

Inaya's head throbbed as she propped her elbows on the desk and buried her face in her hands. Her mother had already signed the consent form that granted Inaya permission to take part in the event, which all nominees were invited to attend. But of course, Inaya had little to worry about if she didn't win. Nominees were invited only as a formality, but only the winner would be expected to actually attend.

Inaya felt sick as she realized what it would mean if she won. She would have to stand before cameras to have pictures and videos of herself publicized for the world to see. If she were to remain the anonymous Muslim she had become at school, she would have to stand before the world without hijab—and humiliate herself and her family. Her friends in Saudi Arabia would most likely be watching, as would her own father, who was drawing from Inaya his own spiritual fortitude necessary to accept Islam.

If Inaya were to do the "right thing" and wear hijab, she would shock the school and Mrs. Ford and humiliate the entire congregation of Future Hope Baptist Church. Mrs. Ford would feel betrayed, Inaya already knew.

Yes, the criteria for the award stated that no one would be discriminated against based on color, race, ethnicity, national origin, gender, or religion; but Inaya already knew that wasn't true.

On their way home, Kayla had told Inaya that Lyrica hadn't even received a nomination letter…yet Lyrica had been nominated by several teachers, administrators, and students. Of course, Kayla didn't know this, but Inaya did—because it was Inaya and Mrs. Ford who made the final list of nominees, a list that Lyrica's name was on when Inaya had completed the list a month before. And there was only one explanation for how it could have been removed…

Until Kayla told Inaya about Lyrica, Inaya hadn't realized the depths of Mrs. Ford's prejudice. Inaya already knew from Mrs. Ford that Lyrica wouldn't be chosen for the Distinguished Student Award, but Inaya hadn't imagined that the faculty advisor would remove Lyrica even from the list of nominees. Was it because Mrs. Ford didn't want Lyrica to even be *eligible* for the Future Hope Scholarship?

The possibility made Inaya weak.

Maybe Inaya should withdraw from the competition herself. This was more than she could handle right then. She could apply for any scholarship. She still had another year of school left.

*There are some opportunities that come only once in life.* The words Sa'ad often uttered came to Inaya right then. *When Allah opens the door for something, don't assume He'll open it again.*

## 15

## The Lesson

*Lazy people work the hardest.* It was something Inaya had
heard many times, mostly as a joke amongst her mother's
friends, but it wasn't until Saturday morning that Inaya
understood it for the first time.

Inaya was in the middle of teaching a lesson to the
children about the traits of the people of Paradise when the
realization came to her. Anyone who insisted on living a life
of sin had to work very hard to avoid the simpler option:
submitting to God.

At the beginning of the academic year, Inaya had decided
to hide her Islam at school, imagining it would make her life
easier. But it had brought her nothing but headache and
hardship. Maintaining the charade of "normalcy" was more
painstaking than simply dealing with whatever challenges
would come along with being openly Muslim, Inaya
realized.

Perhaps those Muslims whose ultimate goal in life was
"normalcy" in the eyes of non-Muslims did not have it as
hard as Inaya. But Inaya had higher goals for herself. Yes,
she wanted to feel normal, but she wanted that normalcy as
a practicing Muslim. It was tiring wearing one face at school
and another at home—and another one in her heart.

Thursday morning Inaya had submitted her scholarship
application and given Mr. Rhodes the permission slip to
participate in the Distinguished Student Award ceremonies
if she won.

No, Inaya still hadn't found the strength to be publicly
Muslim at school, but she wasn't about to give up the
opportunity of a lifetime because of a personal struggle that
would likely be resolved by the time she went to college.

"We'll cross that bridge when we get there," Veronica often said, and these words quieted Inaya's anxiety about the award.

"*As-salaamu 'alaikum.*"

Inaya turned to find Nasra smiling at her, feet from the teacher's desk where Inaya still sat after teaching the Qur'an class.

"*Wa 'alaiku-mus-salaam,*" Inaya said, forcing a smile.

"My mom said we're taking you home today," Nasra said.

Inaya creased her forehead. "Why?"

"She said your mother isn't feeling well or something."

Inaya nodded, remembering that her mother had had a headache when she dropped off Inaya earlier.

"But we're stopping by Kayla's first."

Inaya's eyebrows shot up. "We're going to my cousin's house?"

Nasra smiled, as if realizing something for the first time. "You're related to Kayla? I thought you were just good friends."

Inaya smiled weakly. "Not quite."

"Then I guess you already know about the luncheon she planned."

Earlier that week, Inaya recalled Kayla mentioning something about a lunch at her house on Saturday, but Inaya hadn't paid much attention. She was too distracted by her scholarship dilemma.

Inaya nodded. "Yeah…"

A thought came to Inaya suddenly, sending her heart racing. "Who's going to be there?"

Nasra shrugged. "Just some friends from school, I suppose."

"Will Kayla's parents be there?" Inaya asked.

Nasra shook her head, uncertainty on her face. "I have no idea."

"Teachers?" Inaya imagined she sounded paranoid, but she didn't want to take the chance of anyone from school seeing her in Islamic garb—and she didn't want to take the chance of anyone from her family seeing her without it.

Nasra drew in a deep breath and exhaled. "You don't have to come if you don't want to," she said. "We could just take you home first."

Inaya glanced furtively at Nasra. "If you don't mind…"

"I can drop you off," Nasra said with a shrug. "But we'll have to go by my place first to pick up my car. I rode with my mom today."

There was an awkward pause as a thought came to Inaya. "Do you teach here?"

Nasra shook her head. "I just come sometimes to help my mom. I'm too busy with school, you know?"

Inaya nodded. "Well, if it's not out of your way…" Inaya said, returning to the subject of getting home. "I'm not…dressed for lunch."

Nasra smiled, her eyes telling Inaya she understood Inaya's dilemma—and that she was glad it was no longer hers. "No problem," Nasra said. "I understand."

\*\*\*

"Where were you today?" Chris asked Inaya later that evening after Sa'ad had dropped off Inaya at her father's house. Inaya and Chris were sitting across from each other at the kitchen table, where they had eaten dinner minutes before. "I expected to see you at Anthony's."

Inaya averted her gaze. "Mom wasn't feeling well."

A shadow of concern passed over Chris's face. "Is she okay?"

"It was just a headache," Inaya said.

"That's good," Chris said, his gaze distant momentarily.

Seconds later, Chris grinned widely. "It's a small world," he said.

Inaya met her father's gaze with a confused expression, but before she could ask what he meant, he spoke.

"I met a few of your friends today," Chris said.

Inaya forced a smile, her heart pounding in nervousness. "Really?"

"Well, I already knew Raymond and Lyrica," he said. "But I met a girl named Nasra." He nodded. "She seems really nice."

Inaya's eyes widened. "You know *Raymond*?"

Chris chuckled as he met Inaya's gaze curiously. "He and his girlfriend have been friends with Kayla for years. She invites them to almost every family event we have." He shrugged. "And they used to go to our church."

Inaya smiled beside herself. "That's so weird."

"Why is it weird?"

"I don't know." She shrugged. "Like you said, small world."

There was a long pause.

"Raymond was surprised I'm your father."

Inaya met her father's eyes nervously. "Why was he surprised?"

"It was the first time Kayla mentioned it."

Inaya nodded, her mind a storm of thoughts. She wished she could have been there, if only to hear how her name had come up.

"I've always liked that boy," Chris said thoughtfully.

Inaya didn't know what to say. For months, she had fought feelings of jealousy toward Lyrica, but what bothered her most now was that her attraction to Raymond was beginning to consume her. It hadn't taken Inaya long to realize that Raymond was just being nice to her and that his heart was attached to Lyrica. But what didn't make sense to

Inaya was why this knowledge only increased her attraction to him. She hated that she couldn't control this feeling.

"What time do you have to be home?" Chris asked, looking at Inaya.

Inaya glanced at the clock on the wall. It was just after seven o'clock. "Any time," she said. "Sa'ad said to call whenever I'm ready."

Chris smiled. "Do you mind going with me somewhere?"

Inaya shrugged, a curious expression on her face. "Sure. What time?"

"Now."

Inaya laughed. "Okay."

She was quiet momentarily. "Where are we going?"

"It'll be a surprise," Chris said with a wink. "Get your coat."

Inaya smiled beside herself as she walked toward the coatrack, wondering what the surprise would be.

\*\*\*

Inaya's heart hammered nervously as she sat in the passenger seat next to her father. She was wearing her Islamic clothes, and she could only pray that wherever they were going, it wouldn't involve anyone from school.

When they pulled into a dimly lit parking lot in front of a small building, Inaya's curiosity was piqued.

"Where are we?" she asked.

Chris smirked as he pressed the unlock button and opened his door. "Come with me and see."

Cold wind whipped through Inaya's coat as she followed her father up the small walkway. Through the glass windows of the building, she saw a man with a large beard walking down the hallway, and her heart raced.

Her eyes widened as she noticed the sign on the lawn. It was too dark to read clearly, but Inaya could make out the Arabic writing and the word *Masjid*.

She brought a hand to her mouth as she met her father's gaze.

He smiled back at her and nodded. "I'm ready," he said. He gripped her hand as they neared the double doors of the entrance. "Like you said, 'Why wait?'"

The masjid was sparsely filled as Inaya sat in the back of the small prayer area watching her father repeat the *shahaadah*—the testimony of faith to become Muslim. There were three other men present, but Inaya was the only woman who witnessed her father speaking into the microphone at the front of the room.

Tears filled her eyes as the imam and the other men embraced Chris and welcomed him to Islam.

"All your sins are wiped away," the imam said proudly. "And you are our brother in Islam."

It was almost twenty minutes later that Inaya followed her father out the small building and back to the car. Her eyes were still wet with tears as she sat in the passenger seat. She had so much she wanted to say, but she had difficulty finding the words.

Someone called her father's cell phone before she had a chance to say congratulations. "Too late," Chris said to whoever was on the phone, laughter in his voice, and Inaya thought of Dana. "I told you I wasn't waiting for you."

Chris paused and nodded as he listened to whoever had called. "No problem," he said. "I'll be home in about thirty minutes. You can meet me there."

"I don't know what to say," Inaya said, shaking her head after her father put his cell phone in the compartment between their seats. She couldn't keep from grinning. "That was the best surprise."

Inaya was still smiling when her father pulled into the driveway of his townhouse, and Inaya was only vaguely aware of a familiar car parked next to his.

"Congratulations!" someone called out from the car next to Chris's as he and Inaya got out the car. Inaya glanced behind her as her father went to greet the person whose car door now opened as her father approached.

Unsure if she should be present while her father greeted his friend, Inaya started for the door to her father's home to wait for him there.

"Where do you think you're going?" Chris asked playfully.

Inaya grinned as she halted her steps and turned to meet her father's gaze. "I was just going to—"

Inaya stopped midsentence when she saw Raymond standing next to her father. Chris's arm was around the student ambassador. "Meet your new brother in Islam," Chris said.

Inaya smiled and nodded to Raymond. "My Dad just became Muslim."

Chris and Raymond laughed, and Inaya had the lingering feeling that the two men were sharing a private joke.

"I was talking about Raymond," Chris said as he drew Raymond closer and patted him on the shoulder.

It took a full ten seconds for Inaya to register what her father was saying. She brought a hand to her mouth in surprise, her eyes widening as she looked at Raymond.

"He beat me to it," Chris said, a grin on his face.

"Surprise," Raymond said, his smiling eyes on Inaya.

The wind bit against Inaya's cheek, but she was too distracted to think about the cold. She stared at her father and Raymond, a doubtful expression on her face.

Was this some sort of joke?

"That's why I left school early yesterday," Raymond said. "I wanted to make it official."

"We were supposed to do it together," Chris said, grinning at Raymond. "But the boy said it couldn't wait till tonight."

Inaya still didn't know what to say. The wind swept past again, making Inaya's clothes ripple against her.

"Let's go inside," Chris said. "It's getting cold."

\*\*\*

"I don't know how I'm going to tell Lyrica," Raymond said. He took a sip from the glass of juice he held as he sat on the couch a comfortable distance from Chris.

Inaya glanced up from where she sat on the loveseat across from them, uncertain what to say. But Raymond was looking at her father.

Chris chuckled. "And I don't know how I'm going to tell Dana."

Anxiety knotted in Inaya's chest as she remembered her parents' divorce. Did all relationships have to be sacrificed when a person accepted Islam?

"Maybe Dana will convert too." Inaya's voice was barely above a whisper. She wasn't sure it was her place to make the suggestion.

A part of her wanted her parents back together, but she knew this would mean breaking apart yet another family. She couldn't imagine Abdullah growing up without his father. At least Inaya had had her early years with hers. She couldn't imagine her brother being robbed of that blessing. In any case, there was no sign of Sa'ad and her mother separating, so her desire had been irrational anyway.

Chris looked exhausted all of a sudden, but he maintained a pleasant expression as he shook his head. "I don't think so," he said. "She's a die-hard Christian."

Inaya shrugged and tucked a loose end of her *khimaar* under her chin. "If you love each other," she said, "who cares?"

There was an awkward pause as Chris's gaze grew distant, apparently pondering Inaya's words.

"But love isn't enough," Raymond said, a thoughtful smile on his face as he looked at Inaya. "You need something stronger to hold a relationship together."

Chris smirked and glanced at Raymond curiously. "You sound like an old man," he teased. "I wish I would've known that before I lost my first love."

Inaya averted her gaze. She wasn't used to her father talking openly about his feelings for Veronica. For a fleeting moment, she imagined her parents remarried.

"You live and learn," Inaya said with a grin as she met her father's gaze. "Like you always say."

"Well," Raymond said, humor in his tone, "I prefer to learn then live."

Chris chuckled. "Good luck."

"You don't think it's possible?" Raymond's expression was curious.

"Lots of things are possible," Chris said. "Are they realistic is the question."

They were quiet for some time, and Inaya allowed herself to hope that Lyrica would never accept Raymond's decision. It was a terribly selfish thought, but she couldn't fight the excitement nestling inside her.

"I think it's realistic to learn then live," Raymond said. "That's why I'm not giving up on Lyrica."

Inaya's heart dropped at his words.

"Good for you," Chris said with a nod. "Just know you can't control her heart. She might leave you when she finds out."

Raymond considered Chris's words momentarily. "I think she'll respect my decision."

"Perhaps," Chris said. "But that doesn't mean she'll want a relationship with you."

"That's what friends are for," Raymond said, his tone awkwardly jovial to Inaya's ears.

After a few seconds of silence, Inaya sensed that Raymond's last statement was directed at her. She met his gaze with her brows furrowed.

"Will you talk to her?" Raymond said.

Inaya blinked in confusion. "What?"

"Lyrica," he said. "Will you talk to her?"

"Me?" Inaya rested a forefinger on her chest and contorted her face. "Why?"

"Why not?" Raymond said, leaning forward. "She respects you. I don't think she'll listen if I talk to her."

Inaya shook her head. "I don't know, Raymond. I mean…"

"Why not?" Chris interjected. "It would be a good opportunity for both of you."

Inaya knitted her brows. "How?"

"You can earn some blessings," Chris said, "and she could learn about Islam."

Raymond chuckled. "Well…with Lyrica, we'll just start with God for now."

Chris's eyebrows shot up. "She doesn't believe in God?"

Raymond shook his head. "She's not convinced."

"Wow…" Chris was clearly at a loss for words, a sad smirk on his face. "All this time, I had no idea."

"Most people don't know," Raymond said. "But recently, she's become more open about it."

There was a long pause, as no one knew how to respond.

"To be honest, I don't blame her," Raymond said with a sigh. "She grew up in the church, so she saw a lot of things she shouldn't have. It turned her away from religion."

Chris clasped his hands then leaned forward as he looked at Inaya. "Then it looks like you've got your work cut out for you, sweetheart," he said.

"I appreciate anything you can do," Raymond said, a sad expression on his face as he met Inaya's gaze. "I don't think there's anyone else I could ask."

# 16

## Breaking Point

Inaya threw the covers from herself and sat up in the darkness. The curtains above her bed danced in the cool, late December breeze that drifted through the cracked window. Inaya hugged herself and rubbed her cloth-covered arms as her eyes adjusted to the familiar surroundings.

She glanced at the clock and groaned at the large red digits that glowed 3:02. It was early Friday morning, the last day of school before winter vacation, and Inaya had two final exams later that day.

But it wasn't the English or Calculus exam making her restless. She was fed up with her life. The night before, Inaya and her mother had an argument about a parent-teacher conference that Veronica learned about a week after it had passed. Veronica couldn't understand why Inaya hadn't given her the notice about it.

"What difference does it make?" Inaya had asked as she leaned against the refrigerator with her arms folded in front of her.

"What *difference* does it make?" Veronica eyebrows were knitted in anger. "I'm your mother."

"Don't remind me," Inaya muttered.

The sting on Inaya's face was so sudden that Inaya momentarily wondered what had happened. She stumbled to the side and brought a hand to her cheek as she stared wide-eyed at her mother. Inaya hadn't been slapped since she was child.

The shocked expression on Veronica's face distracted Inaya momentarily from her own shock. Apparently, Veronica was more taken aback by what she'd done than her daughter was.

For several seconds they just stared at each other, Inaya with a hand cradled to her cheek, and Veronica hovering over her, angry breaths warm on Inaya's face. Veronica's glistening eyes betrayed her battle to appear defiant. Shame and regret clouded her gaze.

*"One thing I can't understand,"* Inaya's mother would often say, *"is how Muslims can slap their children."* Veronica would shake her head in disbelief. *"It's not even allowed to hit an animal in the face."*

Inaya averted her gaze, embarrassed to be witness to her mother's transgression.

*"Hitting is one step from abuse if you ask me. That's why I stopped all that foolishness after I became Muslim."*

Inaya's heart was heavy as she sat on the edge of her bed, images from the previous night dark flashes in her mind. The sadness that weighed on Inaya made her too weak to move. She had another few hours before *Fajr*, but Inaya felt no inclination to pray *Witr* before the dawn prayer.

In Riyadh, Inaya had performed the voluntary prayer almost every night, and she'd imagined that she would never leave off the prayer. But now she could barely muster the strength for *wudhoo*. The thought of wetting her arms and face right then made her covet the warmth of her bed.

*"I wish I could live with Daddy,"* Inaya had grumbled after recovering from the shock of the slap.

*"I wish you could too,"* Veronica had said, eyes narrowed defiantly. *"Then you'd come running back, thankful for Islam in your life."*

Inaya had glared at her mother then. *"Daddy's Muslim now."*

It took several seconds for Veronica to process what her daughter had said. Her eyes reflected disbelief, as if she suspected that Inaya was lying.

*"Call and ask him yourself,"* Inaya had said, challenging. *"I was there when he took shahaadah."*

Veronica's expression was difficult to read as she stepped back from Inaya as if wounded. But Inaya thought she saw hurt and confusion in her mother's eyes.

*"You're lying."* Veronica's voice was shaky as she turned her back and walked out the kitchen.

Before Inaya drifted to sleep, she thought she heard crying coming from her mother's room. And she knew it wasn't Abdullah.

\*\*\*

"Nowadays, I don't meet many Christians like you," Mrs. Ford said to Inaya Friday afternoon. Mrs. Ford stood leaning toward her desk as she arranged her belongings after school in preparation for winter break.

Inaya felt anxiety knot in her chest as she sat cross-legged on the floor, labeling some file folders. Inaya frowned and glanced up only briefly, but Mrs. Ford was looking at the pencils she was dropping into a cup.

"To be honest," Mrs. Ford said, "this is the first time I met a young person as committed to God as you."

Inaya felt the beginning of a headache. She wasn't in the mood for this conversation. "A lot of people believe in God," Inaya said, hoping her irritation showed in her tone. "Not only Christians."

Mrs. Ford nodded. "That's true."

The pause that followed was so long that Inaya breathed a sigh of relief. Thank God the woman was shutting up for once. Maybe it was the merry spirit of the approaching holidays that had softened her heart.

"But it's only Christians who follow the truth," Mrs. Ford said.

At that, Inaya rolled her eyes. In a few minutes Kayla would come pick her up, and she could go home. If she could just hold out until then. But Inaya's frustration built until she was indignant. She was tired of hiding her identity in front of this woman. Who was Mrs. Ford anyway?

"That's not true," Inaya said, her voice shaky. "There are a lot of religions in the world."

"Heresy," Mrs. Ford said, waving her hand dismissively. "That's what those religions are."

"Have you ever studied them?" Inaya looked directly at Mrs. Ford, but Mrs. Ford only met Inaya's gaze briefly.

"I'm tired of being politically correct when I talk about God." Mrs. Ford's expression displayed distaste. "We shouldn't have to pretend to be open-minded with non-believers."

"It's about respect," Inaya said, surprising herself by the confidence in her voice. "We don't have to believe what they believe. But we do have to respect them."

Mrs. Ford grunted. "Not with atheists, pagans, and Muslims."

So there it was out in the open, Mrs. Ford's contempt for people like Inaya. Inaya pressed a palm against a box to apply a label, her gaze on her trembling hands. She was unable to hold Mrs. Ford's challenging gaze, but Inaya refused to remain silent on this one.

"Why not?" Inaya's heart thumped until she could feel it in her throat. Her eyes danced between Mrs. Ford and the file boxes. "We can't judge someone just because they don't believe like we do."

"Well, I'll leave the Day of Judgment to God," Mrs. Ford said as she rolled her eyes. "But in this school, I'll do all I can to help fellow Christians."

Mrs. Ford smiled smugly, and Inaya looked away, feeling sick all of a sudden.

"I can't stop this country from destroying itself with multiculturalism," Mrs. Ford said. "But I *can* make sure the Future Hope Scholarship doesn't have the same fate."

*** 

The apartment was unusually quiet when Inaya pushed open the door late that afternoon. She stepped inside and locked the door after she closed it behind herself. In the foyer, she took off her *khimaar* and *jilbaab* and hung them on the coatrack.

The sadness she'd felt early that morning weighed on her limbs as she dragged herself to the bathroom to prepare for prayer. She hated herself for combining *Dhuhr* and *Asr* prayers when she returned from school instead of praying them at their proper times. But no matter how much she told herself she didn't care what the non-Muslim students and teachers thought of her, everything she did showed that she did care.

What didn't make sense to Inaya was why. Other than Mrs. Ford, there wasn't any staff member who Inaya imagined would mistreat her because of her religion. But besides Nasra, Kayla, and the small circle of friends Inaya had known when she first enrolled in the school, no other students or staff knew her faith. "Inaya Donald" was inconspicuous enough—coupled with a "normal" I.D. picture, so it was unlikely that the possibility of Inaya being Muslim had even crossed anyone's mind.

Inaya thought of her mother, and there was a throbbing at her temples. What would her mother do if she found out?

Inaya stepped into the bathroom and turned on the water, leaving the door ajar. She held her open palms under the stream, the cold shocking her senses momentarily. Inaya's eyes met her reflection, and for a few seconds she stared at the girl looking back at her.

*"I appreciate anything you can do,"* Raymond had told her. *"I don't think there's anyone else I could ask."*

Inaya lowered her eyes and mumbled the name of Allah to start her *wudhoo*. She rubbed the now warm water on both hands and wondered at how complicated love was.

Inaya felt embarrassed for putting a word to how she felt for Raymond, but *love* was the only word that unscrambled for her the excitement, confusion, and hope that never left her heart. It couldn't be lust, she thought, because she had no desire to commit sin. But she couldn't deny how Raymond made her feel.

*O Allah*, Inaya's heart cried. *Is that wrong?*

The sound of the phone ringing made Inaya start. She glanced toward the hall then quickly completed the ritual cleansing for prayer. After wiping a wet hand over the top of her socks, she rushed to the living room and picked up the phone.

"Hello?"

"Hey, Inaya. What's up?"

Inaya's heart raced at the sound of Raymond's voice. "Hey," she said more casually than she felt.

"*As-salaamu 'alaikum*, I mean," Raymond said, laughter in his voice.

"*Wa 'alaiku-mus-salaam*," Inaya said, unable to keep from laughing herself.

"Your Dad said you're coming to stay with him for a while."

Inaya's smile faded, forehead creased. "What?"

"He said your mother and stepfather asked if you could stay with him for some time." Raymond's tone sounded uncertain, as if doubting he'd understood properly. "That's not true?"

"I...I don't know." Inaya's mind raced as she recalled the argument with her mother. She glanced about her and wondered where her mother and Sa'ad were right then. A sense of dread came over her.

"Well…" Raymond said, hesitant. "He asked if Lyrica and I could pick you up because he can't come get you."

Inaya's heart constricted at the mention of Lyrica. "What time?"

There was a slight pause. "Can we come now?"

Inaya slapped a hand against her forehead. "Now?"

"It's okay," Raymond said quickly. "Lyrica and I wanted to see a movie anyway, so we can just hang out at the mall. Just give me a call when you're ready."

"Okay…" Inaya said, unable to keep from hating that it wasn't her he'd be taking out. "Is this your number on the caller ID?"

"Yes, it's my cell phone," Raymond said.

"Okay, thanks."

"See you soon." Raymond disconnected before Inaya could reply.

Inaya hung up the phone and placed her hands on her hips as she digested everything. She finally shook her head in puzzlement then started to go pray. She halted her steps when she realized she should call her mother first.

Perhaps her mother could explain the sudden decision to send Inaya to her father's.

# 17

## *Da'wah*

*"Your mother isn't feeling well right now,"* Sa'ad had said to Inaya when he answered Veronica's phone. *"But she says she loves you and just needs some time to herself for a while."*

In Raymond's car, Inaya leaned her head on the back of the seat where she sat behind Lyrica. In the passenger seat in front of her, Lyrica was laughing at something Raymond had said, and Inaya's thoughts drifted as she turned her head to look out the window next to her.

Grayish white snow lined the streets in messy piles under the glow of streetlights, and Christmas decorations suggested a cheer that Inaya did not feel right then.

"Raymond, you're starting to creep me out," Lyrica said. "If I didn't know any better, I'd think you suddenly found religion."

Inadvertently, Inaya lifted her head and looked at Raymond, who turned slightly and met Inaya's gaze with a guilty glance.

*What?* Inaya thought as Raymond looked away and continued to drive. *She doesn't even know yet?*

Inside, Inaya groaned. This little *da'wah* project of his was going to be more than she bargained for. Inaya knew Raymond wanted her to just focus on the concept of God before discussing Islam with Lyrica, but Inaya had no idea Lyrica would know nothing of Raymond's choice when that happened.

Inaya drew in a deep breath and exhaled as she leaned her head back again. As excited as she should have been to have some time to herself and unlimited time with her father (and Raymond), Inaya couldn't muster more than the feeling of subdued acceptance of her predicament.

Was this what her life would forever be like? Tossed back and forth between people who cared about her but had lives of their own? Ironically, everyone saw Inaya's place in their lives as a blessing. Why then couldn't Inaya feel the same about her place in her own?

"How's the BOSS club going?" Lyrica said as they walked up the shoveled walkway leading to Chris's townhouse.

Inaya's hands were deep in the pockets of her coat, and she turned her head at the sound of a dog barking coming from a home they passed. Her gaze rested on the large animal behind a screen door, and she wondered at how a person could leave a front door wide open in the middle of winter.

"It's going okay, I guess," Inaya said.

Lyrica snickered. "How do you like Mrs. Ford?"

"Hey, you made it!" The sound of her father's voice interrupted Inaya's thoughts, and she couldn't keep from smiling at her father, who stood in the doorway of his house.

"Merry Christmas," Lyrica said as Chris stepped aside to let them in.

Chris wore a puzzled look as he exchanged glances with Raymond, but Raymond just shrugged, a smile playing at one corner of his mouth.

"Merry Christmas," Chris muttered, a half smile on his face as he closed the door behind them.

"Hey, where's the tree?" Lyrica said as she shrugged off her coat. Her broad smile suggested her question was a friendly tease.

"I'm not celebrating Christmas this year," Chris said, a polite expression on his face as he took her coat.

"High five to that," Lyrica said, raising her palm to Chris.

Laughing, Chris raised his palm and slapped hands with Lyrica.

"You really don't like religion, huh?" Chris said as he took Inaya's coat and hung it over the crook in his arm on top of Lyrica's coat.

"I'll go get Inaya's bags," Raymond said before Chris could take his coat.

"Not particularly," Lyrica said as Raymond opened the door and stepped back outside. A cold breeze drifted into the room, and Inaya rubbed her arms as she lowered herself onto the couch.

"Why not?" Chris said, a half smile on his face as he opened the front closet and hung the coats inside. "It's not like you created yourself."

"Nope," Lyrica said with a grin. "I give my parents full credit for that."

Chris chuckled as he shut the closet door and sat down on the chair across from the couch. "You're joking, right?"

"No. I'm serious," Lyrica said. "I don't know any other way children are created. Do you?" Her tone was sarcastic as she lifted an eyebrow at Chris.

She shrugged. "Unless we include artificial insemination and in vitro fertilization."

"How could you be so smart but so stupid?" Inaya blurted. Inaya winced as she realized she had spoken her thoughts aloud. *So much for da'wah.*

Inaya felt the shocked expression of her father before she met his gaze, and she hated that she had disappointed him.

"I could ask you the same question," Lyrica said.

Inaya contorted her face as she looked at Lyrica, momentarily forgetting her desire to impress her father. "What's that supposed to mean?"

"It means you sh—"

"Hey, hey, hey." Chris laughed uncomfortably and raised his palms toward the friends. "Let's not get bent out of shape over this."

The room grew quiet as Lyrica lifted her chin proudly and glanced behind her toward the closed curtains. Inaya's heart hammered in angry discomfort, and she dropped her gaze to her nails in an exaggerated attempt to avoid looking at Lyrica. Inaya wished she could go back home right then.

The sound of the front door opening interrupted the silence, and they all looked toward Raymond, who smiled broadly as he deposited Inaya's bags on the floor.

"There," he said. "You're all set."

"Thanks," Inaya mumbled.

What had she been thinking when she agreed to help Lyrica learn about Islam?

"But I'm curious as to why you insist on being an atheist." Chris's tone was pleasant, and he wore a smile as he looked at Lyrica.

Lyrica shrugged. "I don't call myself an atheist," she said. "It sounds too much like a religion."

Chris's eyebrows rose. "Do you ever worry about your soul?"

Inaya glanced in Raymond's direction and saw that his eyes were fixed on Lyrica, as if hoping with all his heart that something was stirring inside her. Inaya sighed silently and turned away. She really didn't understand what Raymond saw in that girl.

"Nope," Lyrica said. But her tone suggested irritation more than conviction.

"Do you believe you even have a soul?" Chris asked jokingly.

Lyrica groaned and stood.

"Raymond, it's late," she said, her voice soft but her annoyance unmistakable. "Can you take me home?"

"Sure," Raymond said too quickly.

There was an awkward silence as Raymond opened the front closet and took out Lyrica's coat.

"Thank you," Lyrica said as she walked to the foyer and put her coat back on.

When Raymond opened the door and Lyrica stepped outside in front of him, he wore a pained expression as he looked back at Chris, apology in his eyes.

"Have a good night," Raymond murmured.

"You too, son," Chris said.

But Inaya remained silent. She couldn't bring herself to acknowledge Lyrica's grand exit, or the reason for it. Saying anything would be like approving Lyrica's behavior.

But Inaya couldn't keep her heart from constricting in fear that her rudeness to Lyrica had cost her Raymond's friendship.

\*\*\*

It was after ten o'clock when the doorbell to Chris's house rang. Inaya was sitting on the couch and holding the remote as she flipped through channels while dishes clanked in the kitchen. Inaya had offered to help her father clean up, but he had insisted that she relax and enjoy herself, though she had no idea how she would manage either one.

"Can you get the door?" Chris called out from the kitchen.

Inaya walked to the front door and looked through the peephole and saw Raymond standing outside. She ran a hand over her hair and rushed to the couch to retrieve the *khimaar* that was lying there. Of course, Raymond saw her every day without the head cover, but Inaya didn't want to announce this to her father. Besides, she had made a commitment to follow the Islamic rules outside of school.

Inaya wrapped the cloth about her head then tucked an edge of the *khimaar* under her chin to hold it in place. She quickly checked her appearance in a passing mirror before making her way to the front door.

"Inaya," Raymond said, a look of surprise on his face when she stood opposite him after the door opened. "Is your father home?"

Inaya motioned her head behind her. "He's in the kitchen."

Inaya stepped aside to let Raymond inside. Her heart thumped as she watched Raymond shrug off his coat and hang it in the front closet. His expression was difficult to read, but guilt gnawed at Inaya as she sensed that he was deeply bothered.

Inaya's heart sank in dread as Raymond walked to the kitchen without saying anything else to her. Inaya thought about how she'd spoken to Lyrica, and she drew in a deep breath before dragging herself to the couch to resume staring mindlessly at the flickering television screen.

"Can I talk to you for a moment?"

Inaya's shoulders jerked in surprise as she looked toward the sound of the voice, the remote control still in her hand. Inaya's eyes were widened when she saw Raymond standing opposite her.

For a split second, Inaya's heart was relieved, even flattered, that Raymond was talking to her. But when she saw his pained expression, the feeling passed. She knew then that Lyrica had talked to him and that he was not happy about what Inaya had done.

Inaya drew in a breath and exhaled as she lifted the remote control and pressed the power button. The noise of the television died suddenly, creating an awkward silence in the room.

"Sure," Inaya said, betraying her true feelings. She didn't feel like talking about what had happened earlier. She wished Raymond could just forget about it.

Raymond sighed as he sat in the chair across from Inaya. "I talked to Lyrica," he said, and Inaya looked away. She had trouble hiding her annoyed expression. "And she says I owe you an apology."

Inaya's eyebrows shot up as she met Raymond's gaze. "What?"

Raymond clasped his hands together and leaned forward, his eyes averted momentarily.

"What happened between you and Mrs. Ford?" he asked after a long pause. His eyes were narrowed in curiosity.

Inaya furrowed her brows at the abrupt shift in conversation. "Mrs. Ford?"

"Lyrica says one of the BOSS members heard Mrs. Ford bragging about you on the phone."

Inaya shook her head, a confused expression on her face. The information didn't surprise her, but she had no idea why Raymond was bringing this up.

"What else is new?" Inaya said dryly.

Raymond seemed a bit taken aback by Inaya's sarcasm. "Doesn't she know you're Muslim?"

For a moment Inaya just looked at Raymond. It wasn't that she didn't understand his question, but she didn't want to acknowledge it. Besides, how was this any of his business?

In all the months Inaya had lived the double life of "regular girl" at school and "Muslim girl" at home, she never had to speak the lie aloud.

But Inaya was surprised that Raymond hadn't known all along. Wasn't it obvious? Why did he think she stopped wearing the Islamic head cover?

"No," Inaya said, surprising herself by her honesty. But she immediately felt ashamed. What would Raymond think of her now?

Raymond slowly closed his eyes and exhaled, as if he had feared this would be her response. He slapped a hand to his forehead and held it there momentarily.

"I'm so sorry, Inaya," he said. His eyes pleaded forgiveness, and Inaya shook her head in confusion.

"Sorry for what?"

He lifted his eyes to the ceiling and groaned, apparently in self-rebuke. "I didn't mean for this to happen," he said, meeting her gaze. "When I asked you to head BOSS, I knew Mrs. Ford wouldn't know you were Muslim, at least not initially."

He shook his head. "But I just assumed after you started working together she would find out."

Inaya shrugged, too exhausted to care. She was the one who should be apologizing, if not to Raymond, then to herself and her family. She should never have tried to live a lie in the first place.

Perhaps this was all a punishment from Allah, she considered. What did Raymond need to be sorry about? He didn't do anything wrong. If anything, she should take it as a compliment that he assumed she was spiritually stronger than she was. She felt bad that she had failed to meet even his meager expectations. After all, letting someone know you're Muslim was the least anyone would expect.

He laughed to himself as he shook his head again. "I had this crazy idea that meeting you would wake her up. I thought she'd finally see how unfair she was being to everyone."

He huffed, a sad smirk on his face. "Of course I knew she'd be impressed by you."

The flattering sentiment made Inaya laugh self-consciously. "What would make you think something like that?"

He sighed, still smiling sadly. "But I had no idea she'd think you were Christian."

Inaya's smile faded, and she dropped her gaze to her hands. She had no idea Mrs. Ford would think that either.

"She's a bigoted hypocrite," Raymond said, the angry words prompting Inaya to look up. He groaned. "She shouldn't even be working there."

Inaya was quiet momentarily, and she hated that she could find no words to defend Mrs. Ford. But she had no idea why she felt any inclination to.

"Lyrica has been begging me to help build a lawsuit against her."

Inaya drew her eyebrows together in surprise. "A lawsuit?"

Raymond nodded slowly and sighed. "Lyrica already threatened Mrs. Ford, but of course, Mrs. Ford isn't taking her seriously."

Inaya shook her head as a thought came to her suddenly. "Is that why Mrs. Ford hates Lyrica so much?"

Raymond smirked. "So you know now, huh? I guess that woman couldn't keep her mouth shut to save her life." He shrugged.

"It's complicated," he said.

Raymond was silent as he leaned forward and rested his forearms on his knees, his expression thoughtful. "But Lyrica can be a bit headstrong when it comes to religion," he said. He chuckled and shook his head. "Even I get annoyed sometimes."

Inaya was unsure what to say.

"But we thought you'd be the best person to tame the beast," Raymond said, humor in his tone.

Inaya creased her forehead as she looked at Raymond. "We?"

"Lyrica and I," he said, a tired smile on his face. "But Lyrica said I should've forewarned you."

Suddenly, everything began to make sense. Inaya glared at Raymond. "So getting me to head this group was just a personal vendetta for you and your girlfriend?"

Raymond narrowed his eyes, as if surprised that Inaya blamed him. "Do you know that that woman has single-handedly made sure that not a single student ever won the Distinguished Student Award except Christians?"

"So?"

"She's using the award to boost support for her *church*," Raymond said as if that justified everything.

Inaya shook her head. "I couldn't care less what she does for her church. I just don't appreciate being thrown in the middle of this."

Raymond sighed. "Well, I'm sorry about that." His tone was subdued. "Lyrica assumed I'd warned you ahead of time."

The sound of music drifted from the television in the kitchen and filled the silence between them.

"I just wish she wasn't so vindictive," Raymond said, speaking more to himself than to Inaya. "Lyrica's lost out on so many scholarships because of her."

Inaya drew her eyebrows together. "I thought Mrs. Ford was only in charge of the Future Hope Scholarship."

Raymond grunted laughter. "She's not even in charge of that one. But she has a lot of connections, so she usually gets her way."

A shadow of anger passed over Raymond's face.

"We knew she was prejudiced," he said. "But we never expected her to sabotage Lyrica's chances at *any* scholarship."

Inaya's chest constricted in anxiety as she realized what this could mean for her personally.

"So if she doesn't know you're Muslim," Raymond said with a sigh, "it's probably best to keep it that way."

"Maybe I should just turn down the scholarship if I get it."

Raymond's eyebrows shot up as he looked at Inaya. "Why? It wouldn't do any good. Mrs. Ford is more proud than Christian. She won't let you just turn down something she's been building up for so long. Especially if she finds out why." He shook his head thoughtfully.

"You'll just end up like Lyrica," he said. "She just walked away, and look what happened to her. Mrs. Ford has plotted against Lyrica so much that there's hardly a teacher or staff member in that school who'll agree to even give her a recommendation letter."

Raymond drew in a deep breath and exhaled as he looked apologetically at Inaya. "So no, turning down the scholarship isn't a good idea. The most you can hope is that someone else wins it."

Inaya shook her head, still upset with Raymond for putting her in this predicament. "Maybe I should just tell her I'm Muslim and save us all the trouble."

Raymond's mouth formed a thin line as he considered what Inaya said. "It might work," he said slowly. "But just be careful."

## 18

# The Announcement

Inaya woke early one Monday morning in late March and felt as if she were coming doing with the flu. The thickness of the comforter that she'd pulled over her face made her breaths warm in the confined space.

Rain pounded incessantly against the window of her bedroom, and she wondered if her mother would let her stay home from school. It was too farfetched to imagine that abdominal cramps would grant her this permission, even though it was "that time of the month." Just two weeks ago, Inaya was home for Spring Break, and Veronica had acted as if that were too much time off from studying.

Inaya coughed to soothe the burning in her throat, and she wondered if she should drink some honey-lemon tea. But the thought of dragging herself out of bed to boil the water and squeeze lemons was enough to discourage her.

In any case, in less than an hour, Kayla was scheduled to arrive. But Inaya imagined that the ensuing thunderstorm would keep Kayla from coming to the door.

"Keep your fingers crossed," Mrs. Ford had told Inaya Friday afternoon, the excitement in her tone leaving nothing ambiguous about what she was referring to. "We're making the announcement Monday morning during homeroom."

For more than two months, Inaya had remained indecisive about what to do about the Future Hope Scholarship and the problem with Mrs. Ford. During the late December night that she had talked to Raymond at her father's house, it seemed that the best option was just being straightforward with Mrs. Ford about her religion. But when Inaya returned to school in early January after winter vacation, the option was no longer appealing.

For one thing, there was no opportunity to bring it up. Though Inaya worked with Mrs. Ford daily and still stayed late after school, they were rarely alone for more than a few minutes at a time. The excess of work because of the approaching annual academic honor's ceremony, Mrs. Ford's role in assisting with the senior graduation, and the BOSS's sudden responsibility to assist Student Council with planning the school prom, made it necessary for at least one other BOSS member to stay after school each day with Inaya and Mrs. Ford.

But even when Mrs. Ford and Inaya found themselves alone for a few minutes, Mrs. Ford gushed about how proud she was that the Christian students were showing their "natural" superiority this year, and how this year's honor's program was going to be "like no other." Mrs. Ford beamed as she shared how her church had sealed an "amazing deal" with a national news company to cover the entire event— something that Mrs. Ford said she hoped would allow her church "to go the next mile."

As if that weren't enough to give Inaya an ulcer, Lyrica's parents, lawyers themselves, were speaking to a team of lawyer friends about filing a lawsuit against the school because of Mrs. Ford's clandestine and illegal actions against their daughter. Of course, Mrs. Ford didn't know this yet because it wasn't yet publicized. But Kayla had told Inaya about it a few weeks ago on their way to school.

*"I don't like it,"* Kayla had said, her face contorted in disapproval. *"It'll just be a big media mess for nothing. Lyrica doesn't even have any real proof against her anyway."*

At the sound of loud pounding on her bedroom door, Inaya fluttered her eyes open. Groggy, Inaya slowly realized she had drifted to sleep.

Frantic, Inaya threw the covers from herself and swung her legs to the floor. She banged the flat of her hand on the clock next to her bed to silence the alarm that must have been blaring for at least fifteen minutes already.

"Inaya!" A second later the door opened, and Veronica's eyes widened in shock as she saw Inaya still in her pajamas. "What are you doing? Kayla is outside."

"I'm coming," Inaya said as she rushed to the closet and pulled clothes from some hangers.

Veronica shook her head. "She's already running late. I'm going to tell her to go on without you."

"I can stay home?" Inaya hadn't meant to sound so hopeful, but she didn't want to miss the opportunity to take a day off.

"What?" Her mother said, wrinkling her nose. "Girl, you better be ready in ten minutes. I'm not letting you play hooky."

Before Inaya could respond, Veronica disappeared behind the slammed door.

It wasn't until Inaya was sitting next to her mother in the car that Inaya realized that the last time her mother had taken her to school was on registration day. Inaya's heart sank as Inaya realized that her mother might find out about her charade. She definitely couldn't take off her *khimaar* and *jilbaab* while she was in the car, as she had been doing each day. But what if Mrs. Ford or a teacher saw Inaya dressed in Islamic clothes?

Inaya silently scorned herself for oversleeping. What had she been thinking?

Ironically, about a month ago, Inaya had hoped she'd be found out. She had grown so tired of the back and forth that she wished her mother would surprise her by stopping by the school or giving one of her teachers a call. Inaya had even purposefully left out a notice about the spring semester parent-teacher conference just so her mother would ask about it. But her mother had been so consumed by her own problems that she didn't even see the note.

"How's school going?" Veronica asked as she gripped the steering wheel and glanced at Inaya, only her eyes visible through her favored black veil.

Inaya forced a smile, and for some reason she thought about how Sa'ad and Veronica had been arguing a lot lately. Sometimes Veronica would ask Inaya to stay with Chris for the weekend, and Veronica went to stay with her own mother for a couple of days.

But recently, Sa'ad had been gone a lot, sometimes for more than a week at a time, and Inaya felt horrible for hoping that he'd never come back. Even Dana and Chris didn't seem to be working out because Dana was furious at Chris for becoming Muslim.

"It's fine," Inaya said before looking out the passenger-side window.

But Sa'ad would always come back home eventually, and he and Veronica would behave like two newlyweds until Inaya grew sick at the sight of them cuddling, giggling, and holding hands.

In the midst of all of this, Inaya began to feel invisible, which was probably why she had started to wish her mother would discover her secret.

But recently, Inaya had decided it was best to keep things as they were. She wanted that Future Hope Scholarship after all, and if that meant Mrs. Ford never knowing she was Muslim, so be it.

When Veronica turned the car into the pathway leading to the school, there were still handfuls of students making their way to the building.

The rain was now a light drizzle, and the sun had started to break through the clouds. The humming of the car engine prompted some students to turn and look in the direction of the sound. Many did a double take at the sight of Inaya's mother—who probably looked like a bona fide terrorist to them.

Mortified, Inaya turned her face away from the window and sank low in her seat. She hoped to God that no one would recognize her through the water-beaded glass.

Veronica glanced in Inaya's direction, and Inaya pretended to be rummaging through her purse. She hoped her mother wouldn't become suspicious enough to ask any questions—or to follow Inaya inside.

Fortunately, Veronica maneuvered the car through the car-packed parking lot instead of stopping near the main door, where school buses still blocked the front driveway of the school.

"Hopefully, you're not too late," Veronica said as she slowed the car to a stop near a side door where some students were making their way up the small flight of concrete steps.

Inaya nodded, but she barely heard her mother as she looked out the window to gauge how "safe" it was to walk from the car to the building while wearing obvious Islamic garb.

Inaya was grateful that she didn't have to walk through the main door, but the side door put her near Mrs. Ford's office. If Inaya wanted to remove her garments in a bathroom instead of the hall, she would have to pass the Student Affairs Office first. But even removing the clothes in the corridor meant she'd be in sight of Mrs. Ford if Mrs. Ford happened to be walking down the hall or standing outside her office door for any reason.

"*As-salaamu'alaikum*," Veronica called out as Inaya opened the passenger side door and stepped outside.

"*Wa'alaiku mus salaam*," Inaya mumbled, dropping her head as she shut the car door. She hoped no one would see her face before she got inside the building and stripped off the *jilbaab* and *khimaar*.

Inaya speed-walked to the side door without even as much as glancing back at her mother. She hoped her mother would assume her behavior was due to being late rather than to Inaya feeling ashamed to be seen with her.

Inaya opened the heavy door and stepped inside, her heart pounding wildly as she quickly surveyed the hall. Some of the few students in the corridor glanced in Inaya's direction upon hearing the door open, but Inaya sighed relief when she realized that none of them were classmates or friends.

The door closed behind her, and Inaya instinctively glanced behind her through the rectangular glass to see if her mother was still outside. Fortunately, it was only a matter of seconds before her mother's car disappeared from view.

From where Inaya stood, she could see that Mrs. Ford's office door was propped open, which meant that Mrs. Ford was either inside or had run a quick errand and would return shortly.

Her face aflame in shame, Inaya turned her body toward the exit door and tugged at the *khimaar* until it hung on her neck and shoulders like a winter scarf. She yanked at the sides of the *jilbaab* until it revealed the outfit she'd chosen that morning in the rush to get ready for school.

Inaya ignored the guilt that gnawed at her as she realized her drab outfit choice was less flattering than the Islamic clothes she was shedding.

Taking a deep breath, Inaya turned and started down the hallway toward the bathroom at the end of the hall.

"Good lord," Inaya heard a familiar voice say, and she looked up to find Mrs. Ford standing in front of her office door holding a manila folder in one hand. "Is it that cold, or are you unwell?"

"I'm not feeling well," Inaya said quickly, running a hand over her hair self-consciously.

Mrs. Ford smiled. "Well, that explains it," she said. "You must be just getting to school."

Inaya nodded. "Yes, I was running late."

"Too bad for you," Mrs. Ford said with a frown, but Inaya knew the faculty advisor was only teasing her. "I went to find you after the announcement, but Mr. Rhodes said you were absent for homeroom."

Inaya's heart raced at Mrs. Ford's reference to the Future Hope Scholarship announcement. Had Inaya won? Inaya was so hopeful that her breath caught.

"Congratulations, Inaya Donald," Mrs. Ford said with a broad smile. "You're our new Future Hope scholar."

# 19

## The Secret

Inaya was so excited she felt like screaming and dancing through the halls.

Following the announcement, Inaya spent the entire week as if in another world. The annual honor's program was next month, and as was the school's yearly tradition, the Future Hope scholar would be the keynote speaker at the event.

Inaya spent nearly every evening after the announcement surfing the internet for the best school speeches in recent history.

Mrs. Ford had personally given Inaya copies of previous Future Hope scholar speeches, and Inaya kept the small stack in a folder on the desk in her bedroom. She had planned to read through each of them, but when she saw the name *Raymond Dirks* at the top of one paper, she lost her enthusiasm.

If there was one thing that could disrupt her peace of mind so completely, it was the sight of his name—or the sight of him.

After their talk in late December, Raymond never asked Inaya about what she'd decided to do about Mrs. Ford, but Inaya sensed that he knew she hadn't gone through with telling Mrs. Ford the truth. And she could tell he was disappointed in her.

*As if he has a right to judge me*, Inaya thought angrily. But the indignant feeling would pass quickly as the true source of her anxiety choked her.

Despite becoming Muslim, Raymond still chose Lyrica over her—even though Lyrica refused to even consider the idea of accepting Islam (or any religion) for herself.

A few weeks ago, Chris told Inaya that Raymond finally divulged to Lyrica his conversion to Islam, and now, conveniently, Lyrica's hatred of religion wasn't as strong as before…though she wasn't religious herself.

"I think he's going to ask to marry her," Chris had joked.

The words were like daggers in Inaya's heart, and she couldn't even meet her father's gaze she was so upset.

"Really?" Inaya had said, unable to muster even the slightest pretence of excitement at the news.

"Well, he says there's no other way for them to be together."

*Bull*, Inaya had thought, annoyed. But she knew it was just her jealousy talking.

Inaya half considered telling Raymond that a Muslim man wasn't allowed to marry an atheist, but whenever she was tempted to confront him, she decided against it. Her motives were not pure, so she should hold her tongue until they were.

But now that Inaya had the Future Hope speech to think about, she could forget about Raymond and focus on more important things.

A part of Inaya knew that she was walking on thin ice with this whole honor's program business. After all, how likely was it that she could keep something as major as this a secret? Past Future Hope scholars were announced in local newspapers and posted on YouTube. And this year Mrs. Ford implied that the coverage might be even more.

"She's full of hot air," Lyrica had said a few days ago during lunch. "She exaggerates for the sake of attention."

The remark hadn't been related to the Future Hope Scholarship national news coverage that Mrs. Ford had shared with Inaya, but Lyrica's remarks did offer Inaya a different perspective on her dilemma.

Yes, it was true that scholarship winners were regularly announced in local and national news—in print, on television, and online. But how popular were these stories really? Even YouTube didn't pose any real threat because most videos there were practically nonentities.

Even Inaya's own internet search on her high school revealed that the school was relatively unknown. The most hits any of its YouTube videos had didn't exceed five hundred, and many had been posted years ago.

Besides, Veronica wasn't a television watcher. She didn't read any print newspapers (other than in the doctor's or dentist office). And she went online only to check her email. Veronica didn't even have a Facebook account because she felt the social medium was inappropriate.

So what was Inaya worried about?

If by some rare chance her mother happened upon the news story, it would probably be years old by then and hence irrelevant. By that time, Inaya would likely be wearing hijab full-time again, and she could simply explain to her mother how difficult covering had been for her as a teenager.

Her mother would be upset, Inaya imagined. But admitting to a past sin was much easier than having it staring you right in the face—through your mother's own eyes—in present tense.

Yeah, Inaya could live with that possibility…if she ever crossed that bridge at all.

But for now, Inaya had to find some convincing reason to stay with her father in mid-April. Then she could sneak off to the annual honor's program—without her mother (or father) knowing anything about it.

# 20

## The Surprise

Veronica groaned as she rushed back to the kitchen to finish preparing the meal. Abdullah, who seemed to have learned to crawl, walk, and run all in the span of just a few weeks, was wreaking havoc on the apartment, and Veronica felt as if she had to be in a million places at once.

Veronica wished she could just let her son run around outside. But living in an apartment robbed her of that freedom, so she had to settle for letting him look out the window in the living room.

The mid-April weather was warm, the perfect day to slide open the patio window and sit with her son on the balcony outside. But Veronica couldn't chance an 11-month-old falling over the ledge.

Normally, Inaya would be home to help her, but Inaya had nagged Veronica to the point of annoyance to spend a week with her father before final exams started in May.

"But he's Muslim now," Inaya had whined when Veronica said she didn't feel comfortable with Inaya spending too much time at his house.

At the reminder, Veronica had reluctantly agreed. She didn't know how genuine her ex-husband's claim was, but it wasn't her place to judge him. But Veronica found his conversion to Islam hard to believe.

The kitchen timer beeped, and just as Veronica reached to silence it, the shrill of the phone sent her heart racing. She sighed and turned off the stove before making her way to the cordless phone affixed to the kitchen wall.

She walked to the living room to check on Abdullah as she pressed the talk button.

"Hello?"

"*As-salaamu 'alaikum!*"

The excited voice sounded vaguely familiar, but Veronica couldn't place it.

"*Wa'alaliku-mus-salaam wa-rahmatullaah*," she said cautiously.

"Is this Veronica?"

"Yes…"

"This is Amal."

Veronica creased her forehead, trying to place the name with a face.

"From the weekend school."

"Oh," Veronica said, laughing. "I'm sorry. I didn't recognize your voice."

"It's no problem," Amal said. "I don't call often, so it's understandable."

"Is everything okay?" Veronica asked, suddenly realizing there might be a problem with Inaya's Qur'an class.

Amal laughed. "Yes, yes, everything's fine. I'm just calling to say congratulations."

Veronica knitted her eyebrows in confusion. "Was there another award ceremony at the Islamic school?"

"No," Amal said, humor in her tone. "I'm talking about the honor ceremony this Friday at the high school."

"At the high school?" Veronica repeated, her eyes following Abdullah as he zoomed past her.

"Inaya didn't tell you she won the Distinguished Student Award *and* the Future Hope Scholarship?" Amal said, pride in her voice. "*MaashaAllah*, it's the first time that a Muslim student has won either award. We're so proud of her."

"Oh…" Veronica reached down to scoop up Abdullah before he knocked over one of her plants, but he wriggled free and took off running again. "She didn't mention it."

There was an awkward pause.

"Really? I just assumed…" Amal's voice trailed, and Veronica's face warmed in embarrassment.

"She's staying with her father this week," Veronica said quickly. She hated the thought of Amal thinking Inaya had purposefully withheld the information from her.

"Well…" Amal said, the excited tone returning to her voice, but Veronica sensed it was forced. "…when Nasra told me about it, I knew I had to give you a call."

"Thanks, I appreciate it."

There was another pause, and Veronica sensed Amal was trying to decide what to say next.

"Nasra is getting a couple of awards too," Amal said. "But she won't be giving a speech or anything."

"Inaya's giving a *speech*?" Veronica couldn't hide her shock.

"Yes, of course. The Future Hope Scholarship winner always gives the keynote address at these ceremonies."

"So you've gone to this…ceremony before?"

"Yes, every year," Amal said, laughter in her voice. "Since her freshman year, Nasra's managed to squeeze at least one award out of the school."

"That's great," Veronica said, but her thoughts were distracted. Why hadn't Inaya mentioned any of this to her?

Veronica thought of how insistent Inaya had been to visit her father, and Veronica's heart fell in the realization that Inaya had probably intentionally kept this from her.

But why? Wasn't this something Inaya would be proud of?

"Do you mind if we do a small piece about Inaya in the Islamic community's newsletter?"

It took a second for Veronica to process Amal's question. "Of course not," she said. "We'd be honored."

"Do you think Inaya would mind?"

Veronica hesitated then chuckled. "Honestly, I have no idea. But I think this is too good to keep secret. It's time Muslims had some good press these days."

"I agree," Amal said. "Besides, the local newspapers and television stations usually cover the event. It'll be good if Muslim media show their support."

Veronica halted her steps in front of the couch. "This event is covered on the *news*?"

"Yes, every year."

"What?" She couldn't believe what she was hearing.

"It's never a big story though," Amal said. "But if you search hard enough, you'll find some mention of it in the middle of the newspaper. Sometimes even a couple of two-millimeter pictures are printed with it."

They both laughed.

"Well," Veronica said, "if the non-Muslims are making even a tiny fuss about it, then Muslims need to make a bigger fuss."

"I don't know how big of a fuss we can make, but I can put a piece in our newsletter."

"Then let's fill the audience with Muslims."

There was a slight pause. "That's an excellent idea!" Amal said finally. "Nasra's on the Student Council. I'm sure she can sneak us a few extra tickets."

"We'll need more than a few," Veronica said, liking Amal's idea. "We want standing-room-only in there." She laughed. "But do see what Nasra can do for us."

"I think this will be excellent *da'wah* for the teachers and parents at the weekend school," Amal said.

"*Da'wah*?" Veronica repeated, laughing. "How would this teach *Muslims* about Islam?"

"Oh you know more than I do how snobbish some Muslims can be," Amal said.

Veronica grew quiet, immediately reminded of how difficult it was for her to get along with Sa'ad's family.

"It's time for Muslims to learn what a real American Muslim looks like," Amal said humorously.

Veronica chuckled beside herself. "If you say so."

"I'll do what I can to fill the audience with as many parents and teachers from the Islamic school as I can," Amal said. "It'll be a nice surprise for them."

# 21

# A Dilemma

"Isn't it obvious?" Anisa's voice asked through the receiver Wednesday evening.

Abdullah was asleep in the small bed Veronica had set up for him in the room she shared with Sa'ad. Her eyes rested on the rising and falling of her son's chest as she sat with her back propped against the headboard. Sa'ad still hadn't returned from work, but Veronica had asked his opinion about Inaya's secrecy before he left that morning.

"I think she wants us to stay out of her life," he said curtly before walking out the door and closing it behind him, leaving Veronica wondering whether he was talking about Inaya or himself.

"No, it isn't obvious," Veronica said defensively as she held the cordless phone to her ear. "I don't see any reason for her to keep something like this from me. She showed me the nomination letter."

"Didn't you say you've never even been to a parent-teacher conference?" Anisa asked. "Don't you see a pattern?"

Veronica rolled her eyes. "That she wants me out of her life?"

Anisa sighed. "Ronnie, have you taken a look at yourself lately? I mean, really?"

"What's that supposed to mean?"

"It means you don't exactly fit the image of the ideal mom."

"*What*?" Veronica glared sideways at the phone as if looking at Anisa herself.

"I didn't mean it like that. I'm talking about from a teenager's point of view. Just think about how you felt when your parents picked you up from school in a beat-up car."

"But we have a decent car," Veronica said. "Nothing like my parents drove."

"But look at *you*," Anisa said. "My husband goes to the school if there are any issues. I don't want my children judged harshly for how I dress."

Veronica creased her forehead as her friend's words began to make sense. She thought back to how quiet Inaya had been on the day of registration, the only day Veronica had entered the school. And how Inaya had looked mortified when Veronica dropped her off the day Inaya had overslept—and how Inaya had never once asked Veronica to visit the school.

*SubhaanAllah.*

Why hadn't it occurred to Veronica before?

As a youth, Veronica had loathed the idea of her mother coming around her friends dressed in clothes that were cheap or out of fashion. How would she have felt if her mother wore a black robe—and a face veil?

Heart heavy in sadness, Veronica begrudgingly accepted the fact that her daughter was ashamed of her.

Veronica had known for some time that there was a rift between her and her daughter. But she loved Inaya more than life itself, and she didn't want to face the possibility that the feeling wasn't mutual.

"But I think you should still go to the honor's program," Anisa said thoughtfully. "Maybe you can just take off your *niqaab* while you're there."

"What?" Veronica contorted her face. "I'd *never* do something like that."

"Why not?" Anisa said. "It's not like wearing the veil is a pillar of Islam."

"But Allah commands us to wear it."

Anisa was quiet for several seconds. "I don't think that's true."

"You *can't* be serious."

"I don't know, Ronnie," Anisa said with a sigh. "But I think it's a bit extreme to dress like that here."

Veronica snorted. "Allah sees us wherever we live. We can't disobey him to please the people."

"I don't think it's disobeying Allah, *ukhti*," Anisa said. "Even the scholars who say it's obligatory allow exceptions."

"But that's only for necessity."

"And you don't think it's necessary to keep a good relationship with your daughter?"

\*\*\*

Veronica lay awake most of the night thinking about what her friend had said. Truth be told, she had been having doubts herself for the last few years.

Living in Saudi Arabia had inspired in Veronica spiritual discontentment that she had difficulty admitting or comprehending. So much of what she had been taught was the lifestyle of the pious predecessors and early Muslim scholars was merely one side of a story—with dozens of other perspectives from the very generation and people of knowledge she thought she was following.

And the issue of hijab was only one of those issues.

Authentic stories reported early Muslim women wearing a variety of fabrics and colors, not only plain black. Some reports revealed early Muslim women, even some female Companions, not wearing the face veil. And most telling, statements from the Prophet himself—and some of his Companions and early Muslim scholars—supported that covering everything except the face and hands was what was minimally required of Muslim women.

Veronica had even attended a class by a respected scholar in Saudi Arabia who'd said:

*The one-piece abaya that you see here is not a requirement of Islam. It is how Saudi women traditionally dress. As for the face veil, there are two valid opinions. Though I personally believe the face veil is obligatory, I believe it is better for Muslim women in the West to uncover their faces than to subject themselves to harm.*

Veronica tugged at the covers until the comforter rested on her shoulder and brushed her chin. The sound of Sa'ad breathing was low and steady.

"Don't be so inflexible," Sa'ad often said. "Otherwise you'll push away those who love you most."

# 22

# Getting Ready

Friday evening, the night of the honor's program, Inaya pulled open the front door to the school, her heart constricted in nervousness. In the backpack that was slung over one shoulder was a folder enclosing her speech and the *khimaar* and *jilbaab* she had worn during the car ride with Kayla.

The noise level rose as Inaya and Kayla entered the hallway, the heavy door closing behind them. Small groups of men and women wearing press badges stood in huddles as if conspiring with each other. Some balanced large video cameras on their shoulders, but none of the cameras appeared to be turned on right then.

"Wow," Kayla said as she followed Inaya toward the crowd. "What are all these people doing here?"

Inaya recognized some members of the administration standing near the press. The administrators were smiling and nodding, obviously proud of whatever tonight would mean for them.

"I know…" Inaya said, her eyes skimming the crowd nervously.

Some members of the administration walked away from the press, and Inaya did a double take when she saw the administrators' pleasant expressions turn to scorn once their backs were to the press.

"Who's responsible for this?" one of them blurted as they rounded the corner to another hall. "I want all the press gone from the premises *immediately*."

Because all awardees had been asked to meet outside the Student Affairs Office, Inaya and Kayla walked down the hall in the same direction as the disgruntled administrators.

"We can't…" someone spoke in a lower tone. "…invite them every year."

"…darn lawsuit, for God's sake!"

At the word *lawsuit*, Inaya and Kayla exchanged wide-eyed glances, and Kayla brought a hand to her mouth.

"Lyrica Spaulding, that's who!" someone said, their tone laced in fury.

Inaya and Kayla looked away from each other. They didn't want the administration to suspect that they knew anything about what was being discussed.

"…should've heard about this before…"

"…can deny the charges…"

"…about Mrs. Ford? She's invited her entire church here…can't ask them to leave…"

The voices became muffled then muted as the administrators entered the auditorium at the end of the corridor and the doors closed behind them.

Inaya's heart raced as she walked in silence next to Kayla. Did Lyrica's family go through with their threat? Was that what all the fuss was about?

The possibility made Inaya breathe a sigh of relief. It was selfish to hope that Lyrica and her family would be the ones harassed by the media, but Inaya didn't want unnecessary attention on herself. The less cameras pointed at her, the less chance her mother (or other Muslims) would discover her double life.

\*\*\*

Veronica stood in front of the full-length mirror affixed to the wall of her room and sighed at her reflection. She wore a navy blue *jilbaab* that hung from her shoulders to her ankles, and a matching *khimaar* framed her face. Sa'ad had bought her the outfit the day before after she'd asked him what she should wear to the honor's program.

*"Be fair to Inaya,"* he'd said. *"No black, and don't cover your face."* Veronica had frowned, but she remained silent.

Besides, she had already resigned herself to this compromise.

Veronica groaned at her reflection then glanced over her shoulder at Sa'ad. "I feel naked."

"If you ask me," Sa'ad said with a shrug from where he stood behind his wife, taking in her new look, "you forfeited the right to dress how you want when you decided to go at all."

"I want to surprise her," Veronica said, her cheerful tone thinly masking the anxiety she felt right then.

"Then surprise her," Sa'ad said, his voice devoid of emotion. "But don't scare her."

Veronica glared at her husband. "I already said I'm not going to cover my face."

"But you're still holding the *niqaab*."

Veronica frowned as her gaze fell to the cloth she held in one hand. "It's hard to part with it."

"You'll be fine," Sa'ad said. "Just don't bring any veiled friends with you."

Veronica was silent momentarily. "Anisa said she'll stay in the hall…with the rest of our friends."

Sa'ad drew in a deep breath and exhaled, and Veronica could feel his disapproval as he looked away from her.

She gritted her teeth in irritation. Would he ever stop judging her?

"I hope you know what you're doing," he said.

"I'm proud of my daughter," Veronica snapped, her tone more indignant than she intended. "Even if you're not."

Sa'ad's lips formed a thin line of disapproval momentarily. "You're proud of *yourself*," he said, his voice rising in upset. "If this was about Inaya, you'd stay home like you know she wants you to. But you just can't resist announcing to world how superior you are."

"*Amal* was the one who arranged tickets for staff at the weekend school," Veronica said defensively.

"Why?" Sa'ad regarded Veronica, his eyes challenging. "So you can make this into another case of why American Muslims are better than the rest of us."

"That's not true."

"Oh come on, Ronnie." Sa'ad grunted and shook his head. "All you ever talk about is how hypocritical 'foreigners' are."

"They *are* hypocritical," Veronica said. "They just assume they're better than us. But they're the ones running from even *looking* like Muslims."

"And you think inviting them to see Inaya get an award will change their minds?"

Veronica huffed and walked toward the door. "I don't think it'll hurt."

"Hurt who?" Sa'ad said, his eyes narrowed. "Inaya, or you?"

Veronica opened her mouth to speak, but the shrill of her cell phone interrupted her thoughts. She waved her hand dismissively and walked over to the bed, where her handbag lay. When she saw Anisa's name on the caller display after she pulled the cell phone out of her bag, she silenced the ringer.

"I have to go," Veronica said without looking at her husband. She dropped the phone back into her purse. "Don't wait up for me."

\*\*\*

"This is insane," Mrs. Ford said, her face twisted in anger as she passed the now large group of students standing outside the Student Affairs Office. When she saw Inaya and Kayla, she did a double take.

"Come here," she said pointing toward them, her expression grave.

Inaya and Kayla exchanged uncertain glances.

"*Both* of you."

Inaya and Kayla looked away from each other, fear written on their faces as they followed Mrs. Ford inside the office. Inaya winced as Mrs. Ford slammed the door.

"What's going on with your friend Lyrica?" Mrs. Ford's eyes were narrowed into slits, her expression accusing as she folded her arms in front of her chest.

"Wh…what do you mean?" Kayla stuttered.

"Is this your idea of a joke?" Mrs. Ford said. "We have more media here than we've ever had for any event in school history. And that includes *before* it became a public school."

A lopsided smile formed on Kayla's face, and Inaya sensed her cousin was getting annoyed with the faculty advisor. "Isn't that a good thing?"

"Oh cut the crap for Christ's sake." Mrs. Ford rounded the desk and slapped her palms on the flat of the desk as she leaned toward the girls threateningly.

"We have almost every news station from the metropolitan area circling this school like dogs and asking us about religious discrimination," she said, her eyes fiery. "And do you know whose name is in the middle of it?"

Inaya and Kayla remained silent, and Inaya shook her head hesitantly.

"*My* name, that's whose!"

Mrs. Ford breathed audibly then let her weight fall into her office chair. The chair rolled away from the desk a few feet, and she leaned back.

"Inaya," Mrs. Ford said after a thoughtful pause, her voice slightly subdued as she met Inaya's gaze. "After the ceremony, I'm going to have you talk to the press…"

Inaya's eyes widened in protest, but Mrs. Ford was looking beyond Inaya, apparently contemplating her own thoughts.

"…and you're going to tell them this is all one big misunderstanding."

"But…" Inaya shook her head, unable to find the right words to refuse. She couldn't risk standing in front of the cameras—on purpose. What if this lawsuit became a high profile, national case? The last thing Inaya needed was to be on the front page of every local newspaper in the city—and in every top news story on TV.

"And you'll tell them you're willing to *testify* to that in court." Mrs. Ford's words were so emphatic they were almost cruel.

Inaya's heart raced as she realized what doing this would mean for her reputation as a Muslim, and that of her family. Veronica would be crushed—and so would Inaya herself.

"But I don't know if I can…" Inaya said, stammering.

"Nonsense," Mrs. Ford said as she stood suddenly and picked up a stack of papers from her desk. Mrs. Ford didn't even as much as look at Inaya as she rounded her desk and started for the door.

"You'll tell them you worked with me," Mrs. Ford said, her tone calm. "And that you never noticed *any*thing even *slightly* religious in our selection process."

Inaya and Kayla exchanged furtive glances.

Mrs. Ford shook her head as if trying to recall something. She looked at Inaya. "And what's that Arab girl's name?"

"Arab girl?" Inaya said, her forehead creased as she met Mrs. Ford's gaze.

"The Muslim one who helps with Student Council."

"Nasra?"

"Yes," Mrs. Ford said, snapping her fingers in recognition as she nodded. "We'll have her talk to the media with you. It'll look good to have Muslims and Christians together tonight."

A grin formed on Mrs. Ford's face as her hand rested on the door handle. "Then these people can see for themselves who's *really* superior."

# 23

## The Honor

Seats in the school's large auditorium were filled to capacity Friday night. Excitement buzzed in the air, silent but palpable. Some men and women stood behind the back row on the lower level, standing alongside the press who couldn't find seats in the now-packed front row reserved for media.

Dozens of the Islamic weekend school teachers, as well as friends of Amal and Veronica, were scattered throughout the auditorium's two levels. The colorful assortment of hijabs added to the already diverse atmosphere. The entire first row was filled with men and women wearing press badges, and their bulky cameras and equipment cramped the aisles on both sides of the rows of seats.

The second and third rows were occupied by awardees from grades nine to twelve, but their awards would be only a preamble to the historic awarding of the Distinguished Student Award and the Future Hope Scholarship. And Inaya, the recipient of both awards, was sitting separately from the students—backstage—preparing for her keynote speech.

Veronica sat in the center of one of the middle rows, and she was more relaxed than she imagined she'd be. She had stressed so much over not wearing the face veil that she had folded her favored black *niqaab* and tucked it into her purse, just to keep it close. But she was surprised by how comfortable she felt without it.

Though Veronica was conscious of how conspicuous her navy blue *jilbaab* and head covering made her appear amidst the public school audience, she felt a sense of camaraderie amongst the Muslim women dressed similarly. Anisa sat a row behind Veronica, wearing her favored all-black *jilbaab* and face veil. When Veronica turned and met her friend's gaze, she found that Anisa had flipped back the *niqaab*, a pleasant expression on her face. Anisa gave Veronica a thumbs-up, letting her know that she was happy to be there, and that she was proud of Inaya.

Veronica shifted in her chair as the program dragged on. She stifled a yawn as she listened to speech after speech. Teachers and administrators droned on about students Veronica didn't know or care about. Names were called out for various awards and honors, and bored, Veronica glanced at her watch. Over an hour passed, and she fidgeted, anxiously awaiting the announcement she had come for.

"And tonight I have the honor to introduce you to our keynote speaker," Mrs. Ford said from the stage podium an hour and a half after the program started.

At these words, Veronica sat up, unable to keep from grinning. She turned to Anisa, and beaming, Anisa made a gesture of upturned hands, reminding Veronica to pray for Inaya's success. Anisa mouthed the words, "Make *du'aa*."

Veronica nodded, still unable to contain her wide smile as she turned forward and murmured a prayer to Allah. She prayed that Inaya's speech would be an inspiration to all present and an opportunity for others to learn about Islam in a positive light. "O Allah," she whispered, "even if only from seeing one of Your servants covered in hijab."

"...and on behalf of Future Hope Baptist Church," Mrs. Ford said, eliciting a rumbling of chatter and commotion from the press occupying the first rows and the repositioning of the men and women behind the video cameras, "I introduce to you this year's recipient of both the Distinguished Student Award and the Future Hope Scholarship...Inaya Donald."

There was a roar of applause, and some of the audience stood, amongst them the teachers at the Islamic weekend school and the friends of Amal and Veronica. Veronica and Anisa also stood for the standing ovation and there were hoots and cheers, inciting in Veronica a sense of pride that made her feel as if her chest would burst.

Tears stung Veronica's eyes as Mrs. Ford looked to her right, the side of the stage where Inaya would emerge to take her place before the podium.

When Inaya emerged, Veronica was momentarily distracted by the gasps of surprise she heard around her, and her heart raced, sensing something was wrong. Then she lifted her gaze toward the stage to see what was causing the confusion…

\*\*\*

Inaya made it a point to avoid Mrs. Ford's gaze as she took confident strides toward the podium. But she knew that the faculty advisor to BOSS would be staring at her dumbfounded…because before this moment Mrs. Ford had had no idea that Inaya was Muslim.

*"Then they can see for themselves who's really superior."*

These were the words that ignited in Inaya a flame of spiritual pride and determination that inspired her to stand before the entire school—and perhaps the world—wearing the very clothes she had tucked away in shame just hours before.

Tears stung her eyes as the audience quieted and she stood behind the podium on stage. Inaya blinked to keep the tears from spilling forth, and she drew in a deep breath in preparation for the speech she had spent so much time preparing.

In that brief moment before she spoke her first words, Inaya was overwhelmed with a longing for her mother. She wished she hadn't been so selfish in ensuring that Veronica would know nothing of tonight's program.

*I'm proud to be Muslim,* Inaya's heart cried, her lips creased in the beginning of a smile as she lifted her gaze to the auditorium filled with people, *and I invite you to share in this love of Allah—in this world and in the Hereafter.*

If there was anything that Inaya wanted to show her mother right then, it was this moment. Despite all Veronica's bickering and lecturing, and Inaya's outbursts of frustration—and their collective anxiety and tearful prayers, Inaya was a distinguished student offering future hope to the world, only because Veronica was her mother.

For all the annoyance Inaya felt with Veronica's rigidity, the only stubbornness that Inaya knew could never change was her mother's overpowering love for her.

Yes, her mother deserved to be there tonight, Inaya thought sadly as she cleared her throat and straightened the notecards in her hands. She whispered a silent prayer to Allah that He would somehow make her mother witness the power of this moment, even if only from a YouTube video or on the local morning news.

Maybe Veronica and Inaya could clip the article from a newspaper and frame it on their walls—and forever hold it close to their hearts.

*I love you, Mommy,* Inaya's heart cried. *And may Allah love you too. Because after Allah, it is only because of you that I am standing here being honored tonight.*

# 24

# Another Reward

There was a roar of applause as Inaya stepped away from the podium. As she walked backstage again, she ignored Mrs. Ford, whose expression of scorn was so pronounced that Inaya could almost taste the woman's disgust.

Inaya halted her steps to pick up her backpack, and she slung it over her shoulder before she continued walking to the exit door backstage. As the door closed behind her, she descended the steps of the empty hall that led to the main auditorium.

Inaya pulled open the auditorium door, and the noise level rose, and she suddenly found herself swarmed by reporters, administrators and friends.

"It appears there was a misunderstanding," a news anchor said, speaking into a video camera. "Earlier reports suggested that the school reserved its most distinguished award and scholarship for only Christian students. But as we saw tonight, both of these awards were given to Inaya Donald, a Muslim girl who we're told enrolled in the school earlier this year after living in Saudi Arabia…"

\*\*\*

Inaya squealed when she saw her mother and Sister Anisa approaching her from the crowd. Laughing, Inaya wedged her way through the swarms of people until she was in front of her mother. Inaya threw her arms around Veronica, and they held each other in a warm embrace.

"How did you find out?" Inaya said after they released each other, Inaya still holding her mother's hands. Inaya was smiling so widely that her cheeks hurt. She was grateful that her mother and Sister Anisa were not wearing their face veils.

Veronica smiled. "Sister Amal called to congratulate me."

Inaya laughed and nodded. "I should've thought of that."

"Hey, superstar!"

Inaya turned to find Nasra approaching her with her arms outstretched. Inaya accepted the hug, and when Nasra released her, Inaya saw Sister Amal smiling at her from behind Nasra.

"We're so proud of you, Inaya," Amal said. "Really, it was such a blessing to be here tonight."

\*\*\*

After chatting with her mother, some friends, and administrators, Inaya rode with Kayla back to Chris's house.

"Did you hear what happened?" Kayla said as she drove down the highway in the darkness. She glanced at Inaya.

Inaya creased her forehead and looked at her cousin. "No." She shook her head. "What?"

Kayla smirked. "Lyrica's pissed off at you."

Inaya contorted her face in confusion. "Lyrica?"

"Yeah, because you ruined her lawsuit."

"*What*?"

Kayla smirked and shook her head. "You showed up in hijab."

Inaya shook her head, confused. "But she knew all along that I was Muslim."

"Yeah, but Mrs. Ford didn't." Kayla raised an eyebrow. "And neither did Lyrica's parents."

Inaya was quiet momentarily. "She told her parents I was *Christian*?"

"Let's just call it the sin of *omission*." Kayla grinned. "I think she just decided not to tell them you weren't."

"And how is that my fault?"

"Well, to win the lawsuit, they have to prove the school favors Christians," Kayla said. "How can they do that now that the world just saw an obvious Muslim take both awards? And from a church-funded scholarship too." Kayla shook her head, smiling. "If anything, this shows how open-minded the school *and* church are."

Inaya grunted. "I wouldn't call them open-minded. At least not if Mrs. Ford has anything to do with it."

"I second that," Kayla said, humor in her tone. "But come next week, I think even Mrs. Ford is going to be thanking you."

"Yeah right. I'll be lucky if she doesn't crucify me," Inaya said, grunting laughter. "No pun intended."

Kayla laughed. "Well, between me and you, I overhead some of the administration talking about suspending her."

Inaya's eyes widened as she looked at Kayla. "Are you serious?"

"Well, I think the term was 'mandatory leave of absence.'"

"Wow. So they know what she's been doing?"

"Who knows?" Kayla shrugged. "They may have known all along and just turned a blind eye." She huffed. "Like schools usually do. But now with all the media attention and threats of litigation, it forces them to at least *look* like they care."

"This is all one big mess," Inaya said with a sigh.

"Not really," Kayla said. "I think it's all for the best." She chuckled. "Who would've known that your last-minute decision to throw on a hijab would solve everything for everyone?"

Inaya was silent momentarily. "Except for Lyrica."

Kayla waved her hand dismissively. "She needs to get over herself if you ask me."

Inaya stared at Kayla. "I would've never expected you to say that."

Kayla shrugged. "She's my best friend, but that doesn't mean I agree with everything she does."

Kayla was silent momentarily. "Okay," Kayla said with a sigh, "I do think Mrs. Ford deserved the lawsuit though. But not the whole school. Lyrica could've solved her complaints internally if she really felt she was being wronged."

Inaya looked out the window beside her. "Maybe."

"Life is life," Kayla said with a shrug. "My parents say there are some things you just have to live with. You can't fight the world every time things don't go your way."

"You sound like my mom," Inaya said, rolling her eyes, a reflective smile on her face. "She always says you have to learn to live with people's imperfections. '*There's only one fight worth fighting every time,*'" Inaya mocked with a smirk. "'*And that's the one against your <u>own</u> imperfections.*'"

Kayla nodded thoughtfully. "Well, she's right."

## 25

# A New Beginning

"Surprise!"

Inaya brought a hand to her mouth, and her eyes grew large as she walked through the front door of her father's house.

Chris, Dana, and Kayla's parents (Anthony and his wife) stood in front of Inaya with their arms outstretched in welcome. A large banner that read "Congratulations!" hung on a side wall decorated by colorful streamers and balloons.

"Oh my God," Inaya said as she stepped inside, laughter in her voice. Kayla grinned as she closed the door behind them. "When did you guys plan this?" Inaya said, shaking her head.

"While you were busy planning how to keep the honor's program secret," Chris said as he walked toward Inaya and drew her into a hug, brushing her forehead with a kiss.

"Sorry about that," Inaya said, her voice subdued as a smile lingered on her face.

"No worries." Chris waved his hand. "I was a teenager once, believe it or not, so I know how it feels."

"We're proud of you," Dana said, appearing at Chris's side and squeezing Inaya's hand. "We really look forward to watching the YouTube video."

"YouTube?" Anthony said from behind them, humor in his tone. "I'm looking forward to the Oprah interview."

They all laughed.

"Why don't we get something to eat?" Dana asked, rubbing her hands together and heading for the kitchen.

\*\*\*

The doorbell rang while Inaya sat on the couch laughing at something her father had said. Kayla and Anthony sat on either side of her while Chris and Dana stood in front of them. They had all finished eating a half hour before.

"I'll get it," Dana said, a smile still on her face as she walked to the door.

"Sorry I'm late."

Inaya looked up to find Raymond approaching the couch, a grin on his face and a wrapped gift in hand.

Inaya stopped laughing, a half smile frozen on her face as she met his gaze. Her heart skipped a beat, and for a moment she forgot about how she had given up hope of anything beyond friendship.

"*As-salaamu'alaikum*," Raymond greeted as he handed Inaya the gift box.

"*Wa'alaiku-mus-salaam*," Inaya replied, averting her gaze, a hesitant grin on her face.

"What?" Kayla said, prompting Inaya and Raymond to look toward her. "You too?"

Raymond smiled and nodded. "Yep," he said, an embarrassed expression on his face. "I'm Muslim now."

"No way!" Kayla laughed.

"Oh can we please avoid the topic of religion for once?" Dana said good-naturedly. "I don't want Chris to get started."

Chris grinned playfully at his fiancée. "Well, you can't avoid the topic of your soul forever, sweetheart."

"Here we go again." Dana rolled her eyes, a smirk on her face. "I focus on my soul every Sunday. Today's Friday."

"Life is short," Raymond said with a chuckle. "Now's as good a time as any."

"How's Lyrica?" Dana wore a pleasant smile as she looked at Raymond, purposefully changing the subject.

"She's good," Raymond said. There was an awkward silence, and Inaya felt uncomfortable.

"Hey, boss," Raymond said looking at Inaya, a smile on his face, "are you up for a quick walk?" He nodded his head toward the door.

Inaya's heart raced, but she maintained her composure. "Sure," she said, shrugging.

"Must be a really special gift," Kayla teased.

"It is," Raymond said, smiling at Kayla as he glanced over his shoulder.

Inaya followed Raymond outside and closed the door behind them. "We can sit here," Raymond said, pointing to the porch steps.

"That was a quick walk," Inaya said jokingly.

Raymond chuckled as he sat on the second step, Inaya following suit, sitting a comfortable distance from him.

"It was just an excuse to steal you for a second," he said.

Inaya smiled to herself, but she didn't say anything. They sat without speaking for some time.

"So I guess Lyrica isn't the best student of religion, huh?" Raymond said, humor in his tone.

Inaya's heart constricted at the mention of Lyrica, but she maintained a smile. "Actually, I'm not such a good teacher."

"I think you are."

Inaya drew in a deep breath as the familiar anxiety returned. So many people expected so much of her. Sometimes she wished people could just see her as the normal human being she was. Why did Raymond imagine she could help him maintain his relationship with Lyrica, of all things? Didn't he see that Inaya had feelings of her own?

Inaya grunted. "Well, I doubt Lyrica thinks so."

Raymond shrugged. "So what? That doesn't mean she's right."

Inaya started to respond but realized what she wanted to say was better left unspoken.

Yes, Raymond was right. Just because Lyrica thought negatively of Inaya didn't mean it was true. But it did mean that Inaya had failed Raymond in what meant the most to him.

And that meant that Inaya had failed in what meant the most to her.

"I'm sorry I couldn't help," Inaya said quietly.

Raymond drew in a deep breath and leaned back slightly. He was silent for some time. "I'm sorry too," he said finally.

The sadness Inaya felt at these words was so overwhelming that she was glad she was sitting. She blinked back the moisture in her eyes and looked away, mortified that she was so affected by Raymond's disappointment. What was wrong with her?

"I shouldn't have put that burden on you," he said regretfully. "I should've taken it on myself." He drew in a deep breath. "Like I should've faced Mrs. Ford."

"It's okay," Inaya said. "Allah is the best planner."

Raymond nodded as his gaze grew distant. "I wish I had as much faith as you."

Inaya sighed. There it was again. As flattering as his words were, Inaya didn't like being put on a pedestal. She was full of faults like everyone else. She wasn't perfect—which was why she couldn't calm the desire she felt for Raymond right then.

"Raymond," Inaya said finally, her voice exhausted, "I don't have as much faith as you think. If I did, I wouldn't have put on one face at home and another at school."

He creased his forehead and glanced at her curiously. "What you do mean?"

Her eyes widened slightly as she met his gaze. "This," she said, tugging on the cloth of her fuchsia *khimaar*. "Didn't you notice I wasn't wearing it to school?"

"Yes," he said, his expression confused. "But that doesn't change who you are on the inside."

Inaya shook her head, realizing that Raymond would probably never understand. "Maybe," she said with a sigh. "But it *does* show how weak I am on the inside."

Raymond looked perplexed, but he shrugged. "I'm still learning a lot about Islam, so I'm sure you know more than I do. But I don't see why it's such a big deal. If anything, it shows how weak the school is. It's obvious you felt forced to change your appearance."

Inaya considered his words momentarily then glanced at him curiously. "What makes you say that?"

He drew his eyebrows together and met her gaze. "Am I wrong?"

Inaya looked away, her thoughts drifting to how difficult it had been to live a double life. But she had wanted to fit in at school; no one had forced her to feel that way.

"I don't know," she said finally.

They were quiet, and their gazes and thoughts became distant momentarily.

Raymond broke the silence and handed Inaya the wrapped gift. "Just a little something to say congratulations," he said, a subdued smile on his face.

Inaya's spirits lifted slightly as she accepted the gift, but a sense of sadness tugged at her heart. Why couldn't she abandon her fairytale dreams? Would she ever get over her desire to one day marry Raymond?

Inaya held the box, unsure what to do. She was curious to see what was inside, but she didn't want to offend Raymond by opening the gift in front of him.

"Open it," he said, humor in his tone. "I want to see your reaction."

Inaya glanced at him suspiciously, a smirk on her face. "Why?"

"You'll see."

Curiosity piqued, Inaya tore the cellophane paper from the box and set the wrapping next to her on the cement steps, a grin on her face. She opened the flaps of the cardboard and removed the white tissue. She creased her forehead as she took out the folded white cloth that appeared to be a simple T-shirt.

She smiled. "Thanks."

Raymond laughed. "Unfold it, and look at it."

Grinning curiously, Inaya unfolded it, and a small badge fell on the step at her feet, distracting her. She leaned forward to pick it up and saw that it was slightly worn and read "Student Ambassador."

She drew her eyebrows together and chuckled. "What's this?"

He laughed. "You don't remember?"

She creased her forehead and glanced curiously at him. "Is this yours?"

He nodded. "I was wearing it when we first met."

She laughed. "Thanks," she said, her face growing warm. "I'll treasure it."

"Really?" He sounded surprised.

"Of course." Uncomfortable with the possibility of being asked to explain further, she lifted the T-shirt from her lap and held it up to read the imprint on front: *Keep the faith, girl, and, insha'Allah, we'll meet in the End.*

It took Inaya several seconds before she registered why the words sounded so familiar. Her eyes widened and she looked at Raymond. "How did you…?"

"Nasra," he said, a smile on his face. "She said one of your friends from Saudi Arabia shared it with her mother."

Inaya laughed, shaking her head. "Wow, *maashaAllah*. I had no idea you knew about that…"

"I did my research," he said with a smirk.

They were quiet momentarily as a thought occurred to Inaya. "But why?"

Raymond drew in a deep breath. "Honestly?"

Inaya chuckled. "Well, if it's not too much to ask."

Raymond was quiet for so long that Inaya grew concerned that she had asked too much.

"Because I didn't want to lose hope."

Inaya nodded as she considered what he had said, but she realized she had no idea what he meant.

"You know why I wanted you to talk to Lyrica about Islam?" Raymond said.

Inaya's chest constricted in dread. She didn't want the reminder. "No," she said, her voice barely above a whisper.

"Because I wanted her to be like you."

The words were so unexpected that Inaya laughed. "Yeah, right."

"I'm serious." There was humor in his tone, but Inaya detected a trace of nervousness. "I knew I could never…" He huffed then shook his head. "Never mind."

"Could never what?"

He looked at Inaya suddenly, his eyes pained. He seemed frustrated for some reason.

"Don't you get it?"

Confounded, Inaya creased her forehead. "Get what?"

Raymond drew in a deep breath and exhaled as if trying to gather his thoughts.

"You know the story of Abu Talha and Umm Sulaim?"

Inaya narrowed her eyes. "It sounds familiar."

Raymond smiled, but his expression remained subdued. "Read it when you get a chance," he said. "It's the story your father told me before I became Muslim."

"*MaashaAllah*," Inaya said, smiling. "Is it what inspired you to convert?"

Raymond laughed. "I guess you can say it was the final push."

"Then I have to read it," Inaya said, shaking her head as she smiled.

"Well, remember me when you do, okay?"

Inaya chuckled, unable to shake the lingering feeling that she was the butt of a friendly joke. "Of course."

Raymond stood. "Then you'll understand the T-shirt better. It's what I've been telling myself." He sighed as Inaya stood too, a confused expression on her face. "Even when I didn't understand why," he said.

Inaya nodded. "Okay…"

"I just hope you don't find it offensive," he said as he opened the door and stepped aside to let Inaya in front of him.

"Why would I find the story offensive?" Inaya said, chuckling.

Raymond grinned. "Let's talk about that after you read it."

"How's everything with Lyrica by the way?" Inaya said quietly as Raymond followed her inside and closed the door.

"We broke up," Raymond said sadly.

"I'm sorry," Inaya said, bringing a hand to her mouth. She was surprised by how sad she actually felt. "I didn't know."

Inaya shook her head, sad for Raymond's pain but unable to quiet the hope nestling in her own chest. "Why?" she said.

"Honestly?" he said, a smirk forming on his face as he nodded his head toward Inaya. "The truth is in your hands. Literally."

She glanced down at the T-shirt she was still holding. *Keep the faith, girl, and, insha'Allah, we'll meet in the End.*

Inaya broke into a grin, and her eyes widened as she met Raymond's gaze. He grinned and looked away as he walked into the living room to join everyone else.

Maybe marrying Raymond one day wasn't a fairytale after all…

# epilogue

*Looking back, I think I know what my mistake was. I thought being a good Muslim meant you didn't do anything wrong, at least not on purpose.*

*But now I know, if you're human, you're going to make mistakes. You're going to do wrong—sometimes on purpose. And you're going to get confused and weak.*

*But what's most important is, no matter how crazy life gets, nothing makes you lose faith altogether.*

*Because that means losing everything.*

*And even if things get so bad that all you have is your emaan, that seed of faith that keeps you Muslim, that's something.*

*In fact, it's more than something. It's what makes all the difference…*

*In this world and in the Hereafter.*

# ABOUT THE AUTHOR

Daughter of American converts to Islam, Umm Zakiyyah, also known by her birth name Ruby Moore, is the award-winning author of the *If I Should Speak* trilogy and the novels *Realities of Submission* and *Hearts We Lost*. *Muslim Girl* is her second juvenile fiction story after *A Friendship Promise*.

Umm Zakiyyah's books have been used in schools and universities in America and abroad for multicultural and religious studies. She writes about the interfaith struggles of Muslims and Christians, and the intercultural, spiritual, and moral struggles of Muslims in America.

She currently resides in Washington, D.C.

Visit **ummzakiyyah.com** to find out more about the author.

CPSIA information can be obtained
at www.ICGtesting.com
Printed in the USA
FFOW05n1646050515

9 780970 766786